THE BORING DAYS AND AWESOME NIGHTS OF ROY WINKLESTEEN

By
Sally Dill

Thinkbutton, Inc.
Charlotte, North Carolina

Thinkbutton, Inc.
Charlotte, North Carolina
thinkbutton.com

Visit the author's website at:
sallydill.com

ISBN-10: 0-9996671-0-6
ISBN-13: 978-0-9996671-0-1

To Tristen:
Merry Christmas!
Glad you joined our
school family this year!
♡-
mrs. H

To all the nightlifers of the world—
and a very special one in particular.
May the darkness always help you find your way.

CONTENTS

THE BORING DAYS
AND AWESOME NIGHTS
OF ROY WINKLESTEEN

CHAPTER 1

THE LAST DAY OF SCHOOL

Roy's clock read 2:11 a.m. As usual, his parents thought he had fallen asleep hours ago. As usual, they were wrong. He was never asleep when they checked on him. He only pretended to be so that they would leave him alone. Roy liked the nights to himself, and he never had a problem finding things to do when everyone else seemed perfectly happy doing nothing.

On this particular night, Roy sat at his desk writing a list—an extremely important list. His entire summer depended on the words he wrote on the faint, blue lines before him that seemed to tease the part of his brain where ideas were supposed to emerge. Nevertheless, Roy knew that without a list, his parents were destined to fill the next 74 days with activities not worthy of the faintest mumble, much less the "How I Spent My

Summer" presentation due at the beginning of the next school year. Although the assignment was always the easiest of the year, it was, by far, the most important for every student enrolled in the Dodson Mills school system. An awesome summer break guaranteed any student at least a two-rung leap up the popularity ladder—even for Roy. Each year the stakes got higher, and by middle school, everyone had to create a corresponding poster to hang outside the classroom. Pictures don't lie, so exaggerating an aunt's above ground swimming pool into the French Riviera or transforming a trip to the zoo into an African safari was no longer an option.

Without a doubt, this year's presentation had sealed Roy's fate as grand, supreme loser of fifth grade. Sixth grade, however, was going to be different: a new school, a new assignment, a new life. Roy was on a mission to stuff his summer with so much awesomeness that his status at school would extend beyond the ranks of the most popular eighth grader. He just had to get his list finished:

1. CLIMB A MOUNTAIN (KILIMANJARO)

2. SWIM WITH SHARKS

3. BUNGEE JUMP FROM A HOT AIR BALLOON

4.

Roy sighed at the meager contents on the blinding, white page before him. Maybe he was a loser. As he stared at his frozen pencil, beckoning him to write something—anything—his mind wandered back to last summer.

FOCUS, he thought, shaking his head in desperation. Still, he found it impossible to forget such an unmemorable summer filled with sore throats, tonsil surgery, a princess birthday party, and a gushy wedding. He was so sick the month of June that he couldn't play soccer or go to camp. He barely saw his best friend and spent most of his time in bed or playing with his little sister, Melonie, who Roy preferred addressing by the scientific(ish) name: Annoyous bratticus. That's because it was her fault everyone called him Roy. His real name was Charles Royston Winklesteen III, but when his sister was younger, she couldn't pronounce Royston, so she called him Roy and, somehow, it stuck. So, as far as he saw it, two could play that game.

He spent most of July recovering from having his tonsils removed. Oddly enough, surgery was the best part of his summer—all the ice cream he could possibly eat and less time with his little sister. Like most stained and sticky kindergartners, adults considered Melonie a traveling Petri dish of multiplying germs forbidden to come within arm's reach of his healing mouth. On the other hand, his parents hovered around him like crazed gnats, and Roy eventually reached a point where time with Melonie would've been a welcome change.

Forgetting the whole experience proved quite difficult because his mom displayed the plastic bottle containing his extracted tonsils on the kitchen counter like a new cooking appliance. She showed them to anyone who was brave enough to look. Even more embarrassing, Melonie named them Roofus and Stanley and told everyone the lifeless blobs were her pets.

He didn't understand the fascination. To Roy, they looked like nothing more than two bloated, cherry-flavored jellybeans floating aimlessly in some snot-like substance. Fortunately, when no one was looking, Roy managed to hide the disgusting bottle deep in a cabinet, behind all the soup cans with bizarre combinations of ingredients no one ever dared to eat or confessed to wanting in the first place.

By the time August rolled around, school shopping, a cousin's out-of-town wedding, and planning and preparing for Melonie's sixth birthday party gobbled up the few remaining weeks of summer. And, if any of his friends found out his parents made him dress up like a prince for the party, he was finding a new family. No one should ever have to put up with such humiliation.

It's not that Roy didn't love his family. His dad, Charles Winklesteen, was a fun guy to hang out with, when he had the time. Roy enjoyed trips to the home improvement store and watching his dad's eyes bug out every time they passed a new tool. Because it was one of the few places his parents both felt worthy of the family's extra spending money, Roy and his dad went there a lot. His mom, Helen Winklesteen, a precise and loving woman, thought their house always needed some type of improving, and his father was more than happy to oblige.

As for Melonie, she always needed something, especially attention from Roy. He had to admit, he did use her admiration of him to his advantage. She would do and get anything for him. The only problem was, she didn't know how to do much and was usually too puny to get anything he needed. Nonetheless, Roy didn't want to change who his family was, just what they did as a family.

He skimmed down his list. Maybe swimming with sharks was a bit extreme and dolphins were a more reasonable choice. Besides, Melonie would likely scream and squirm the whole time, scaring the sharks away. Then again, what kind of poster did he want? One filled with underwater shots of sweet dolphin smiles or close-ups of razor sharp teeth? Sharks . . . definitely sharks. Besides, Shawn Lee rode a dune buggy in the desert with his family. Will Hopkins got to hike through the Australian outback. Cynthia Owens spent a month at space camp. And Eliza Pruitt's summer with her Secret Service uncle was too secret to talk about, so she passed around a framed letter excusing her from the assignment. Needless to say, the entire class actually listened to their presentations.

Finally, a vision came to him:

1. Climb a mountain (Kilimanjaro)

2. Swim with sharks

3. Bungee jump from a hot air balloon

4. Camping and ziplining through a jungle (Amazon)

His list was just long enough to start a family conversation—something his parents lived for. Roy's mom thought communication was the glue that held a family together. Roy wasn't sure if glue was necessary, but he knew an outstanding adventure was exactly what the dull, predictable, safe Winklesteens needed.

Satisfied with his late night efforts, Roy knew he had to get some sleep. Today was not only the last day of school—it was destined to be the best day of school. Nothing could prevent him from missing out. He had waited all school year for it.

He turned off his lamp and managed a glimpse out his bedroom window. Even in the moonlight, his neighborhood reminded him of a tray of cupcakes topped off with colorful icing swirls, each gripping a two-cent, plastic prize. Like the tray of cupcakes, the neat rows of houses offered a delightful arrangement of identical parts where slight differences suggested the illusion of individuality. It was obvious the rest of his family and the neighborhood were an excellent fit for each other. Roy, on the other hand, didn't fit in anywhere.

He never told anyone he preferred moonlight to sunshine. The sun arrived each morning with blinding rays of light and smears of dainty color, while the moon whispered its arrival against the flat, black sky. Life depended on both, but Roy seemed to relate better to the easy-going moon, politely fulfilling its role without all the drama.

He was a diehard nightlifer. And as far as he was concerned, daylifers had no idea what they were missing. They wasted the quiet solitude of the night letting their subconscious control their dreams, while he spent the stolen hours consciously planning a way to make his dreams come true. Convinced he was the only one awake, the nights were one thing Roy didn't have to or want to share with anyone.

So he thought.

As his eyes locked in on the window's lifeless view, something looked out of place. Not only did it look peculiar, it moved. On top of one of the shallow rooftops, one street over, perched a very large bird. Freakishly large. Maybe it wasn't a bird. But it did have wings stretched out on either side of a dark, slender body. The wings were definitely bird like. The body, not so much— human perhaps?

Roy grabbed his binoculars from his desk drawer and focused on the shadowy creature long enough to watch it leap from the gabled roof and soar wonkily into the night sky and out of sight.

Roy didn't know what he had seen. Maybe he was hallucinating. Maybe it was nothing but an eye floater. Either way, he was obviously tired, and his brain was making up stories to keep him awake. Sleep, that was all he needed. So he crawled into bed. Closing his eyes was the easy part. Drifting off into dreamland, though, was virtually impossible.

His brain wouldn't leave him alone. It kept banging on his skull, forcing him to think instead of sleep. His body didn't want to move, but he knew his mind wouldn't shut up about what he'd seen until he at least attempted to calm his curiosity. Therefore, he knew what he had to do.

Roy kicked off the covers, sat straight up, let out a big sigh, and made his way back to his desk. He rubbed his eyes and leaned toward the window. He blinked a few times and stared directly at the rooftop. He saw exactly what he thought he'd see—nothing. He stared at the sky, and it revealed the same thing—nothing. He even grabbed his binoculars and saw the exact same thing through them—nothing. He fell back into bed and tried to ignore his nagging neurons. He wasn't very successful. And when he did finally doze off, the questions hunted him down in his dreams. What was it? Why was it there? Was it something he should fear? Did anyone else see it? Was it a person? Was it an animal? Was it both? Was he going crazy?

Roy couldn't take it anymore. He returned to his desk and stared out his window until the night transformed into day. Usually, the arrival of sunlight put Roy in a bad mood, but today he felt relief from the humdrum view before him. His neighborhood couldn't have looked more normal, and the question-making part of his brain became bored with the lack of inspiration his eyes presented. Roy's thoughts switched gears, and he was able to channel all his energy into making the most of the day's activities.

He got dressed and hung out in his room until he was sure the rest of the Winklesteens were downstairs in the kitchen. It was important that every family member be around when he revealed his list of adventures. Roy zipped into the kitchen, where his entire family was eating waffles.

"You're running late, sleepyhead," his mom said with a smile and a sip of her tea. "You must be going through a growth spurt. You seem to need more sleep lately."

"I dunno." Roy hurried past his mom towards the refrigerator. He secured his list of adventures with a ceramic magnet he'd made at school and then sat down to eat.

"What's that on the fridge?" His father looked beyond his newspaper.

"It's a list—a list of adventures we can go on together this summer." Roy kept his expression serious. "Last summer was pathetic. We need to stop being such a boring family and do some fun stuff together like all my friends do."

"Boring?" His dad folded up the paper like it had arrived and placed it next to his plate. "I didn't realize we were boring. I thought we could do some painting and fixing up around the house." He gave a wink to his wife. "Maybe we could get some new tools."

"Yes, that's all we need . . . more tools." She smirked back. "Maybe we could visit Uncle Bill this summer. He hasn't seen you kids in a while and he lives close to the beach."

"I wanna go to the beach!" Melonie announced, yanking Roy's list off the refrigerator. "Swim with sharks! Are you crazy, Roy?" She tossed the list on the kitchen table. "Let's go to the beach. That's kinda on Roy's list."

"Well, I wouldn't mind the beach," his dad added as he got up from the table. "Swimming with sharks? I don't know about that—maybe dolphins instead?"

"Yea, they're cute and slimy, like Roy's tonsils." Melonie looked in the direction of where the disgusting container used to be on display. "Mommy . . . dolphins."

"We'll see," his mother insisted with a sigh. "For now, let's try to get through the last morning of the school year. We have all summer to—"

"I'm gonna miss the bus." Roy grabbed a waffle off his plate and headed towards the door.

"Wait . . . Roy . . . what about a kiss?" His mother leaned in, giving him a big smack on the forehead. "Have fun at Nicholas' this afternoon."

"Will you play house with me tonight?" Melonie pulled on his sleeve.

Roy wiggled his arm away from Melonie, snatched his list from the table, and hurried out the door. He stuffed the list in his pocket and barely caught the bus.

On the ride to school, Roy's best friend, Nicholas, chattered the entire time. Roy didn't listen. He was too busy trying to figure out how the best day of the school year was starting off no different than any other day: completely unmemorable. How could his family blow off his list? What were they? Robots, totally incapable of comprehending anything outside their preprogrammed little world? No way was he going to let his summer break consist of nothing more than home improvement projects and a trip to weird Uncle Bill's to swim with "cute" dolphins. Tonight, he would demand a family meeting and insist the rest of the Winklesteens make serious plans for a summer that would guarantee him a one-way ticket out of Loserville.

Once at school, Roy took a break from his list and savored the day. He ate fistfuls of candy and chips, and his teacher awarded him with a kite for receiving the highest score on the state math exam. The celebration continued with soccer in the park and a cookout in his best friend's backyard.

Roy returned home to find his family winding down with the evening TV lineup. A meeting was definitely in order, but his stomach was twisting angrily and his tired, watery eyes made him look like he was actually sad school was over. His list would have to wait. All he could think about was sleep. The last thing he wanted to do was deal with the rest of the Winklesteens. He wasn't in the mood.

His pitiful attempt to sprint past the family only resulted in more commotion, and his mom's radar quickly honed in on him. After a momentary debriefing of the day's activities, Roy finally dragged himself upstairs and retreated to his room. He plopped down on his tightly made bed, pulled his crumpled list out of his pocket, and ironed it with his hand. His eyes shifted over to the packaged kite leaning against his bed. His brain wasted no time reminding him of the few moments of oddness that had occurred almost 24 hours earlier. He glanced up at his half-opened window. It was now officially nighttime, and as tempted as he was to look, his body finally beat his brain. Within seconds, Roy's mouth flopped open, and he fell into a deep sleep.

CHAPTER 2

THE FIRST 21 HOURS

Bawoof . . . *bawoof, bawoof.* Roy tumbled out of his bed and onto his hands and knees. *Bawoof.*

His clock read 1:57 a.m. Very rarely did he hear a dog barking so late at night, or so early in the morning, depending on one's perspective. For Roy, no sunlight meant nighttime. He loathed anything having to do with mornings.

Dizzy and confused, he staggered to his feet, tripping over his kite, then leaping towards the direction of the noise. His heart was pounding. He leaned over his desk and opened his window as far as it would go. Right as the neighborhood came into focus, the barking abruptly stopped. Roy scanned the area for any hint of a dog or the reason for its barking. Not surprisingly, the view was nothing more than it always was: lifeless and typical.

Annoyed a yelping dog interrupted his desperately needed sleep, he pushed away from the window and sank into his desk chair. He closed his eyes and relished the silence. Within a few minutes, the damp night air blanketed him with an energizing chill and he sat straight up, excited to take advantage of his time alone.

He wasn't sure what to do. He picked up his list, now resting on the floor, and reviewed the contents. Did he have enough options? It couldn't hurt to add a few more. It wasn't like he didn't have the time. He returned to his chair and spun around towards his window. And that's when he saw it—again.

He fumbled for his binoculars and pressed the eyepiece hard against his face. With a few swipes up, down, and side to side, he managed to narrow in on the movement.

Like the night before, a strange figure balanced precariously on a roof ridge one street over. In angelic fashion, the short, stocky wings stretched out on either side of the body. Roy no longer doubted the shape was human. It was trim and masculine looking, dressed in head-to-toe black with some sort of vest to the thighs. The person appeared to be wearing goggles and an old-timey helmet.

The wobbly figure trotted down the roof ridge,

shoved off the edge, and dipped down towards the ground before darting up and over a tree line and out of sight.

Roy dropped his arms into his lap. His head began to throb as he listened to his brain dig through piles of fact and reason. What he thought had been a weary-eyed vision, straight from Greek mythology, was real. Trying to blink as little as possible, Roy locked his eyes on the neighbor's rooftop. It seemed pretty clear that the person who flew off the roof had some connection to the house and would hopefully return. But after an hour crept by, Roy began to think he was wasting his time. He couldn't ignore the possibility that his neighbor might end the flight in another location.

Just as he was about to give up, a flash of black streaked across the bluish-gray sky. Roy jumped up with his binoculars to see the winged person come in for a running, tiptoed landing. In a matter of seconds, the man had the vest off and folded onto itself. With a tug of a shingle, a section of the roof opened up like a hatch door, revealing an entrance to the attic below. The man, with his wings, dropped down into the opening and shut the hatch.

Roy felt his way back into his chair and sat painfully still. His eyes and wide-open mouth felt about the same size. He had a neighbor who strapped on a set of wings and flew like a bird. How could he not have known this before now? Were there more? Maybe there was a secret club of flyers. Obviously, flying like a bird was something only available to nightlifers. If daylifers flew with wings, it would be impossible to keep it a secret.

Tingling with energy, Roy twirled around and popped out of his chair only to trip, once again, on his kite. He grabbed the package and ripped it open. The flimsy black, yellow, and white flier landed against his legs and spread open. He took the time to examine the contents from every angle. A kite was nothing without the wind and string. And up until a few moments ago, Roy thought the only way humans could fly was with planes, parachutes, jetpacks, or gliders. Now, he knew differently. If his neighbor could fly like a bird, then why couldn't he? Roy figured he had all summer to find out, and that was exactly what he planned on doing.

He dropped the kite on the floor and rolled onto his bed. Soon, the sun would begin its grand entrance, which meant all the daylifers would arise from their blissful slumber and into the slog of their daily routines. For Roy, it was time to sleep. He was sure nothing exciting would be happening for a while.

Undoubtedly, he'd forgotten what day it was.

"Wake up . . . wake up!" a voice yelled out. Roy lifted his head off his pillow to find Nicholas jumping up and down on his bed. The jostling and bouncing was making him queasy.

"C'mon, get up. Let's go do something. It's summer— no schoooooooolllllll!" Nicholas leapt off the bed, pulled the covers off Roy, and wrapped them around his neck like a cape.

"Give me second," Roy said, his voice hoarse from only four hours of sleep. Suddenly, it dawned on him. Today was the first day of summer, and he wasn't about to waste it sleeping. He sprung out of bed and wrestled with Nicholas for a moment, threw on some fresh clothes and followed his best friend downstairs to the kitchen, where Melonie and his mom were finishing their breakfasts.

"Roy, will you help me get this knot out of my doll's hair?" Melonie asked, wedging herself between the boys.

"Ugh . . . get outta here Melonie." Roy pushed his sister aside, rolling his eyes so Nicholas could see.

Nicholas snorted and politely addressed Roy's mom,

"Mrs. Winklesteen, my mom said it was okay for me to hang out at the park all day. Can Roy come?"

"Sure, but drop back by for lunch. I'm making—"

"Okay." They each grabbed a piece of bacon and ran out the door.

On the way to the park, Nicholas rambled on about finding enough friends to get a soccer game going. Roy listened, sort of. He was having a hard time focusing on his day when all the real action was clearly happening at night. Roy wanted to tell Nicholas about his flying neighbor but questioned if telling anybody, even his best friend, was a good idea. It was a hard story to believe. First, Nicholas was a daylifer and would never understand why Roy was up so late. Second, a neighbor that flew with wings, like a bird—seriously? For now, he would keep his late-night discovery to himself. Besides, if there was some type of secret nightlifer flying club, he didn't want to expose their secret, he wanted to join them. For now, keeping quiet seemed like Roy's best option. Excited to begin his summer, he tucked away the questions regarding his past two nights and spent the whole day with his best friend.

He returned home that evening right in time for dinner. Anxious to begin his surveillance of the flying neighbor's house, he finished eating before his mom even had a chance to sit down. Just as she cut into her perfectly square slice of lasagna, Roy backed his chair slowly away from the table. He hoped his sister's mindless jabbering would prevent the rest of the Winklesteens from noticing his departure.

"What happened to your list Roy?" His dad gestured towards the refrigerator.

"Oh . . . yeah, it's in my room somewhere," Roy said. "We'll talk about it later."

"But aren't we going swimming with the dolphins?" Melonie asked with a mouth full of peas.

"I'd better go take a shower." Roy stood up and started towards the stairs.

"A shower?" His mother dabbed the corners of her mouth with her napkin. "What about your list?"

"I need to work on it some more," Roy yelled out from the stairs. "We'll talk about it tomorrow."

After his shower, Roy hid in his room. Melonie banged on his door a few times, but he bellowed out that he was reading and wanted to be alone. He knew if he mentioned the word "reading," his parents would keep Melonie away from him. Even so, he had to be more careful about future methods for avoiding his family. Volunteering to take a shower or reading for fun would certainly make his parents suspicious.

In the dark of his room, he studied every aspect of the flying neighbor's house. The two-story structure towered over the neighboring one-story homes. Although it fit in stylistically, the house definitely stood out. Not because the neighbor was trying to get noticed, but because they clearly wanted to be left alone. Unlike all the other homes, whose shrubbery felt like open arms welcoming all that approached, the flying neighbor's tall fence and large trees seemed to hug the house, as though protecting it from all that wandered too close. It didn't look creepy or haunted, but it was pretty clear that the person who lived there didn't want anyone knocking on the door selling cookies. It shouted, "KEEP OUT"—but in polite way.

And that made the view outside Roy's window even more fascinating.

Convinced the neighbor would emerge long after all the daylifers were asleep, Roy set his alarm for 1:50 a.m. For now, he would try to get some rest.

CHAPTER 3

THE NEXT 64 HOURS

Bawoof, bawoof, bawoof. Roy's eyes popped open. He dove to his window and aimed his binoculars at the flying neighbor's roof. Even though the barking continued, Roy could have discovered more life in a cemetery. He scanned the tidy yards for signs of a dog, but an abundance of shrubbery hid the noisy source. Roy's clock read 1:32 a.m. He turned off his alarm that was set to go off in 18 minutes. Still early, he thought. He rested his head on his hands and locked his eyes in on the house. The barking eventually stopped. Roy inspected the neighbor's roof. Even through his binoculars, the hatch door was undetectable. Simply knowing it was there made Roy's heart feel like it was trapped under an icy lake, pounding desperately to break through. Would the mysterious flying man make an appearance tonight?

Roy didn't have to wonder for long. The neighbor's house seemed to wake from the dead as the attic window lit up and a distorted human shadow undulated across the small, sloppily draped panes. Like the door to a UFO, the roof hatch opened slowly. The light from the attic shot directly towards the sky. The neighbor poked his head out and looked left and right. He crawled out onto the roof, holding the winged contraption over one shoulder so it rested on his back. Once completely out, he lowered the hatch and hung the wings from the chimney.

Roy angled his spy-like stance closer to the window as he watched his neighbor back into the vest and fasten everything together. Next, the man lowered his goggles, adjusted his helmet, and slid his arms through straps on the wings. While trying to lift the contraption off the chimney, the lanky figure almost tumbled down one side of the roof. Luckily, a sharp lean to the right prevented any potential disaster.

As the man trotted down the ridge, Roy noticed his speed and steps seemed awkward. During the other two takeoffs, he took one large, last step and thrust himself off the end of the roof. Tonight, he shortened his final step, which caused his foot to completely miss the roof edge. There was no lunge toward the sky, but instead a stumble off the edge, followed by a death dive to the ground.

"Oh, no!" Roy gasped, pressing the binoculars against his face so hard it hurt. He was relieved the trees prevented him from witnessing what he thought was his neighbor's horrifying end.

Still, the man wasn't done. He reemerged above the trees and zipped back up above the roofline. With a tilt to the far right, he circled around toward his house, barely missing a clump of trees before crashing, chest first, into the chimney. The man bounced back onto the ridge and began sliding down the roof. The right wing got caught on a vent cap, saving the struggling figure from tumbling to a bone crushing demise. Roy sucked in his breath. Should he get someone? Call for help? Tell his parents? His neighbor could be seriously hurt.

Before Roy could make a decision, the man struggled to his feet and leaned against the chimney. He unstrapped the vest and balanced the wings across the ridge. He kicked the vent, then reached down and opened the hatch. Within seconds, the neighbor and his flying contraption vanished down the hole.

Roy didn't know what to think. Had what he'd witnessed been a success or a failure? His neighbor could have died, or at least been badly injured. Yet, he saved himself. Roy wondered if a mishap of this sort had happened before. Any sane person had to know the risks of strapping on a set of wings and leaping off a roof. Regardless, even Roy knew adventures worth pursuing came with risks, which was precisely the reason he wanted to swim with sharks and not dolphins. Roy finally concluded that the man had succeeded at flying; he merely hadn't flown as far as he had planned. He wasn't going to give up on his neighbor and was hoping his neighbor hadn't given up on himself.

Roy watched the house until the man's attic window went dark. He thought maybe his neighbor would attempt another flight, but the situation didn't look promising, so he crawled into bed.

Roy tried to sleep, but he couldn't get the death defying flight out of his mind. Maybe his neighbor realized he was hurt once he climbed back down into the attic. Maybe he would have to spend weeks in the hospital. Maybe the fall had damaged the flying contraption beyond repair. Maybe the man's life had flashed before his eyes, and he decided flying like a bird was no longer worth the risk. Maybe the man would leave the wings out by the road for trash pickup and Roy could retrieve them.

Roy tossed and turned. He couldn't stand the fact that he was going to have to wait 24 hours to find out whether or not his neighbor would fly again. Even 24 minutes sounded too long. Roy had to find a way to kill some time, so he hopped back out of bed and returned to his desk. He flicked on his lamp and searched for something to do.

Something caught his eye. He stood up and walked over to his calendar hanging next to his corner window. In one of the squares labeled "Friday," he'd written "family reunion." He ran the dates through his mind and came to a dreadful conclusion. The family reunion was tomorrow, an hour away and for two whole nights. How could he have forgotten? It was all his mom had been talking about for the last month. UGH! As if 24 hours wasn't agonizing enough, the thought of 72 hours made him want to destroy every clock in the universe.

Roy's mind went blank. The rest of the night seemed like one of those dreams where all you could remember about it was the fact that you had dreamed. He only seemed to get his senses back after his mom entered his room around 9:00 a.m., put a stack of clean clothes on the bed, and told him he had to be packed by 4:00 p.m. Roy's body did what it was told to do, but his mind refused to go anywhere. It would stay in front of his window waiting for the rest of Roy to return a few days later.

For the next 48 hours, Roy tried to do as little thinking as possible. Somehow, he managed to make it through the tsunami of relatives, hugs, questions, food, pictures, and conversation. He tried to plant a smile on his face, but every cousin was into games and toys too embarrassing for a sixth grader to admit to liking, and all the adults seemed to talk about was politics and weather. The best part about the entire event was saying goodbye to everyone. Like his mom, Roy even shed some tears (although his were of joy) as everyone packed up and drove their separate ways. The weekend was finally over, and it wouldn't be long until he was back in front of his window.

He was just about asleep when his father interrupted the low hum of the car wheels as they spun down the interstate. "Roy, have you finished your list?"

"Um . . . I never found it . . . forget it . . . I was being stupid," Roy replied, hoping to put an end to the "list" conversation. He didn't need his family to go on an adventure. He had one unfolding one street over from their house.

His mom turned around and gave Roy the typical smile all mothers manage when their children blurt out ideas that all adults universally agree are impossible. Then, she uttered one of the top 10 quotes every adult uses to confirm their parental wisdom: "There's no such thing as a stupid idea." Roy wasn't sure if it was the car ride or the conversation, but either way, he felt nauseous.

Fed up with the "list" conversation as well, Melonie stated her opinion loud and clear. "We don't need Roy's list. We're going to Uncle Bill's to swim with the dolphins."

"Well, we aren't sure Melonie. The whole family has to vote on what to do," his mom said softly, although with a look that undoubtedly conveyed she meant business. "That's how the Winklesteens make decisions."

Not a fan of the democratic process, Melonie whined about family plans the rest of the way home. Roy shut his eyes and tuned his entire family out. He already had his summer (nights) planned, and the rest of the Winklesteens weren't included.

CHAPTER 4

THE NEXT 169.5 HOURS

For the next six nights, Roy fell into a tedious routine of waiting and watching. Without fail, his neighbor emerged from the hatch around 2:00 a.m., returning at varying times, but always before 4:00 a.m. Although often shaky, his takeoffs never included the heart-stopping blunder that had occurred the week before. Each night of spying revealed a little more about the shadowy neighbor.

Roy's daytime plans were also right on track. For the entire week, he attended an all-day math camp with Nicholas. Roy loved numbers. Equations made more sense to him than sentences. He saw math in almost everything, even in the famous art he had learned about during a museum field trip. He had no desire to paint or sculpt like an artist. Instead, he understood pieces of art by using equations to reveal their proportions and relationships, and that was all he cared to know about the subject.

Roy was proud of his ability to manage his very different daylifer and nightlifer schedules. As for his nightlife, it was time to take his investigation to the next level. He had to get a closer look at his neighbor's house and at his neighbor. Roy decided Sunday was the ideal day to seek out more information. He painstakingly calculated every detail of the mission.

After he was sure all the other Winklesteens were asleep, Roy made his move. Thanks to his mom, he had an easy way out of the house without anyone knowing. Right outside his corner bedroom window was a fire escape. It was really nothing more than a rope tied to a sturdy oak branch. But it was the ideal fire escape for a young boy. His dad had installed it after his mom insisted Roy needed a way out of the house in case his parents couldn't get to his room at the opposite end of the hallway during a fire. According to his parents, it was a fire escape and, therefore, only to be utilized as such.

To Roy and Nicholas, a rope hanging from a tree outside his window only to be used during a fire that was probably (hopefully) never going to happen was a waste of perfectly good rope. Both boys used the fire escape whenever possible. As for Helen Winklesteen, all she needed to know was that her son was safe. It was a winning situation for everyone, and Roy was always careful not to jeopardize the benefits of his parents' overprotective tendencies.

Tonight, Roy was taking the fire escape without his best friend. After arranging his pillows and a kick ball under the covers, he flung his pack over his shoulder. The sleek, black bag contained the usual spy gear like binoculars, a flashlight, a pad of paper, some pencils, and a camera. He stepped onto the rugged, wooden chest under the window and gently pushed up the sash. The air outside was moist, giving the summer air a false chill. He reached for the nearest branch and grabbed hold. With his other hand, he felt for the rope, looped several times around a bigger branch. He patted the rope until he found the frayed end and then began a series of backwards tosses over the gnarled limb.

Finally, with one last toss, the ground was in reach. Roy squeezed the rope with both hands and leapt off the windowsill. His straight, dark hair got tangled up in some leaves as he swung back and forth trying to secure his legs around the floppy line. The cracking of branches and creaking of the rope seemed to make more racket than Melonie rearranging her plastic kitchen play set. Roy froze in place until the swaying finally slowed. His hands traveled one over the other as he made his way down and onto the grass.

Roy was already breaking a sweat. He was excited in a way he'd never felt before. He crept around the front of the house and inspected his parents' bedroom windows. Both were dark. He darted down the driveway, crossed the street, and hunkered behind a bush he'd scoped out earlier. It was the best spot to observe the flying neighbor's house and his own house, especially his parents' windows.

He sat cross-legged, behind the bush. The sharp, flashing numbers on his Ooberleeben survival watch read 1:25 a.m. While he waited, he took a moment to admire the exceptional timepiece secured around his wrist. His dad had bought the watch during a trip overseas. Roy smiled every time he looked at it. Not all the kids at school noticed him, though they always stopped to admire his watch. Swiss-designed for grownups, it wasn't only a watch—it was also a flashlight, a compass, flint, and an emergency signal with a tracking device. All the disk-shaped tools were precisely stacked underneath the watch face, like a hamburger with all the fixings. When Roy needed to use one of the tools, he pivoted out the desired disk from underneath the face.

Purely amazing, Roy thought. The entire unit was a tad bulkier than most watches, but its size only attracted the attention it deserved. Even though the Ooberleeben didn't have a cool laser beam that could cut through walls or a sturdy, retractable cable that enabled Roy to scale a building, it was, by far, the next best gadget for any spy to have.

Although annoying at times, he was glad his parents were safety freaks. If they were as laid back as Nicholas' parents were, he wouldn't have the fire escape or the Ooberleeben. He had to make sure his parents never found out about tonight, and since he'd taken the risk, he needed to make the most of it. He was prepared to do whatever necessary to ensure he returned home with more information than when he left.

So, he waited. And waited some more. 2:30 a.m. came and went, same for 3:00 and 3:30 a.m. The attic window was dark, the hatch door closed, and the flying neighbor was nowhere in sight.

Covered in goose bumps, tired and frustrated, Roy stretched out his cramped legs and stood, hunched over, behind the bush. As he scoped out the other neighbors' homes for any signs of life, he noticed a glimmer of light coming from some downstairs windows beyond the flying neighbor's tall, wooden fence. Perhaps tonight the action was happening on the first floor and not the attic or roof.

CHAPTER 5

THE NEXT 15 MINUTES

Roy had about two hours before the neighborhood started humming and his dad's alarm clock officially rang in the morning. He spent the next few minutes glancing back and forth between the distant gaps of the fence, hoping for a glimpse into his flying neighbor's world. A real spy would never give up until successful, and Roy's night had been far from successful. At that instant, he felt like the only choice was to move in closer.

He wrapped his pack around his shoulders and crept between two adjacent houses and up to the wooden fence. While partially hidden behind a very scratchy bush, Roy attempted to look between the splintery slats. The flying neighbor's first floor lights were on, but the thick hedge made it difficult to determine anything else. He hesitated. Had Nicholas been with him, they would've dared each other to go further. It was always easier to be fearless when you had a friend watching you.

Keeping his eye on the light, Roy crouched along the fence. He made his way around the side of the secluded yard, continuing to follow the fence until the lofty, wooden house stared straight down on him with its sinister-looking windows. As he approached the front corner of the fence, he noticed a row of faintly lit windows on the side of the house. Roy grinned with relief. Breaking into the flying neighbor's backyard was no longer going to be necessary.

He attempted his best cat burglar creep to the bottom of the closest window. Grabbing the windowsill with both hands, he extended his legs just enough to see inside. Boxes of every size filled the space. Beside a lamp balanced on an overturned bucket, a plate with a half-eaten sandwich provided the only indication humans currently occupied the home. Roy had never considered the possibility that more than one person might live in the house.

Overcome with a flood of bravery, Roy completely straightened his legs so that his face reached the dead center of the lower pane. He pressed the sides of his hands against the cool glass and tucked his head between his fingers. He was sure he detected movement in an adjoining room. Were the shadows those of his flying neighbor?

Bawoof! Bawoof! Grrr . . . Bawoof . . . Bawoof! In one swift push, Roy toppled to the ground. A dark, very large dog dug its claws into his chest. The fierce beast stared Roy down.

Grrr . . . Bawoof . . . Bawoof! Every bark and growl shook the saggy skin on either side of the vicious creature's jaw. Roy knew he was face to face with the source of the late-night barking. Roy froze in fear. He didn't know which was worse—the fact that he was going to get caught sneaking out, or the fact that a grungy dog was going to chew him to bits. While he contemplated his fate, a slimy line of drool seeped out one side of the creature's curled jowls and slowly made its way towards Roy.

"Shirley . . . get off. Shirl, c'mon now . . . get inside and hush," a gruff, whispery voice commanded. *Bawoof!* The dog slowly backed off Roy. But not before a slimy line of slobber broke free from the dog's left jaw flap and landed directly in Roy's nose and across his lip.

"Shirley, get in the house . . . now." The indistinct figure jerked the dog by its collar. Roy sat up and wiped the revolting drool from his face. The stranger bent down and stared into Roy's eyes. The light from the window illuminated the man's slender, ruddy profile and red, wavy hair.

"What are you doing out here . . . so late?" Roy was yanked to his feet. "Are you spying? What have you seen?" Roy couldn't speak. "Well . . . what's your problem?" Roy still didn't respond. The man grabbed Roy's scrawny arm and dragged him through the side door of his house. He slammed the door, flattened Roy against the wall, and bent down so their noses exchanged air.

"Who are you? What do you want?" The man tilted his head from side to side as though he were studying every pore on Roy's face. "Can't you speak?"

Roy felt paralyzed. He knew the warm nostril air was that of his flying neighbor. "I was—"

Grinding his teeth and looking meaner than his dog, the man snarled, "Was what?"

"I only wanted to get a closer look."

"A closer look?" The man lowered his lids until his eyes were as narrow as paper cuts. "A closer look at what? What do you think you know—what DO you know?" His fingernails cut into Roy's arm. "Have you seen something?"

"I s-saw you the other night. You can fly with wings."

"So . . . what if I can?" The muscles in the man's jaw popped out as he ground his teeth together. "It's none of your business. Who have you told?"

"I—I haven't told anyone." Roy turned up the volume in his voice. "Not even my best friend."

"Could this night get any worse?" The man released Roy's arm like it was a rotten piece of meat and then paced back and forth, rubbing his temples. "Now what am I going to do? Out of all people—a kid—a bleepin' kid."

"What's wrong with me being a kid? I told you I haven't told anyone, and I'm not going to," Roy said.

"What's a kid doing up so late anyway? Don't you have some sort of bedtime or something?" The flustered neighbor inspected Roy from head to toe. "Like I asked already, who ARE you anyway?"

"My name is Roy, Roy Winklesteen. My house is one street over—the two-story, blue one." He pointed to his right, hoping his directions were in check. "My parents don't know I'm up so late. They never do. I was sitting at my desk and saw you fly the other night—through my window. I think you're amazing," Roy said, hoping a compliment would calm the man down. "Are there others who fly like you . . . at night . . . with wings?"

"Don't be ridiculous. There are no others." The man

scrunched up one side of his upper lip and stared at Roy as if he'd never heard such a dumb question. "I made the wings. They're my invention. No one has ever been able to fly like a bird—except me—and I plan for it to stay that way. Is that clear?"

Pop . . . spur . . . pop, splish.

"Now . . . what?" the man grumbled. He looked behind him and back at Roy. "Stay right here . . . I'm not done with you yet." The man disappeared into the next room. Some mumbling and commotion soon followed. Roy was too afraid to move. Shirley, as he'd come to know her, was still staring him down. Even sitting, the top of her head easily came to Roy's chest. She had to be the ugliest dog he'd ever seen. Her short, gray fur, sprinkled with brown and dull white spots, made her look like she'd been mud wrestling with a squirrel. Her flappy jowls hung well below her mouth with a steady stream of drool seeping out both sides. However, what really made her so unsightly was her half-chewed-off ear. It was supposed to come to a point, like the other one, but the point was gone and all that remained was a raggedy stump with pinkish scars and random bald patches. The gangly animal sat staring at Roy. And the more Roy stared back, the less ferocious she looked.

After a while, he managed to rally enough nerve to make his away around the ugly dog and towards the racket occurring in the next room. Shirley didn't seem to mind. She continued to sit, only turning her head to follow Roy's movements. He made his way to the arched opening leading to the kitchen. The man stood in front of the stove, frantically tending to a large, steaming pot with streams of white goo oozing down the side.

"I thought I told you to stay put," the man said, never taking his eyes off the pot. "You've seen too much." The man looked right at Roy and kept on stirring. "Now I have to figure out what I'm going to do with you."

Roy was no longer scared. He was terrified. What did the man mean by that statement? What did he have to figure out? Roy panicked. Maybe there had been others who had discovered the man's secret, and now they were locked away in a dank cellar right below Roy's feet. Maybe he'd buried the unfortunate, curious souls in his secluded backyard. Maybe that pot of stuff the man was stirring contained the brains of other people he'd caught spying on him.

STOP, Roy yelled to himself. He and Nicholas should have never watched that monster movie marathon. His imagination was starting to get the best of him. Calm down, he thought. The man didn't look scary—maybe a little strange—but not scary. He was probably like his dog, "all bark and no bite."

No matter what, Roy wasn't going to go quietly. "I told you, I haven't—I won't tell anyone. I'm sorry I was spying. I only wanted to know more about how you flew. Where you went. How you invented the wings," Roy hesitated and then suggested in his most respectful voice, ". . . and if it was something I could do at night . . . maybe?"

"Are you joking, kid? You? Fly?" The man looked like he was going to self-combust. "Do you know how long it took me to make the wings precisely the right size—out of the right material? It's not something anybody can do. Or has the privilege to do, as far as I am concerned."

"Sorry, I thought—"

"Yeah . . . well, you shouldn't think so much." The man tossed the wooden spoon he was using on the counter and stared Roy down. "Now you've created a huge mess for me. No one—I mean no one was supposed to know about this."

"I didn't mean to find out about it. All I did was look out my window and there you were—on your roof." Roy tightened his stance. "I know I'm only a kid, but I'm pretty sure anyone who saw what I saw would've wanted to know more."

The man sneered back at Roy. "It was two in the morning! Do you know how many people are up at two in the morning . . . looking out their window?"

"I don't know . . . at least one . . . I guess," Roy said.

"Yeah, you're right—one stinkin' kid who's blown everything I have spent my life creating."

"How have I blown anything? For the hundredth time, I WON'T tell anyone." Now more disappointed than scared, Roy turned around and headed towards the door he'd been dragged through minutes earlier.

"WAIT . . . hold on kid." The man bowed his head and sighed. "I guess we need to work something out. I can't let you go like this. You know my secret, and there's nothing I can do to undo that. So you need to prove to me you won't tell anyone. Besides . . . I guess it's not the end of the world if one person knows," he admitted. "It might actually be kind of nice to talk to someone about everything. Sometimes, I feel like I'm losing my mind."

Roy whirled around with excited eyes. "I'll listen. I want to know everything. I think you must be some sort of genius or something. If I'd invented a way for humans to fly like birds, I would tell the world. You could probably make millions, maybe billions of dollars! You know . . . sell your wings so everyone could fly and—"

"NO. Like I told you . . . no one needs to know," the man said. "I know that might sound weird. But trust me, I have my reasons."

Roy stood in the opening, perplexed. "Whatever you want . . . I'll be happy to hear whatever you want to tell me. I'm great at keeping secrets. Ask my best friend. I've kept a really big secret of his . . . even from his parents . . . and they should probably know."

"Really?" the man asked, his eyes widening. "What . . . what's the secret? You can tell me. I don't know you . . . or your friend . . . or his parents. So, why would I ever tell?" He stepped towards Roy and began interrogating him like a curt police inspector. "Is it bad? Did he cheat on a test or something? Or . . . I know . . . he fed his pet fish so much it exploded."

Roy didn't appreciate his neighbor's lame attempt to be funny. He was turning out to be no different from every other adult he knew. None of them took him seriously either.

"Can't be that bad . . . you're not old enough to do anything bad," the man said.

"I didn't say it was anything bad."

"Okay. So, it's not bad." The man leaned down, once again, to stare directly into Roy's eyes. "C'mon . . . your friend would never know I know. I'm good at keeping secrets, too. Remember . . . I had a really big one until you looked out your window."

Roy was getting frustrated. He didn't know how to reason with this guy, so he gave his most logical response. "It's not my secret to tell."

"If it's not bad, then why is it a secret anyway?" The man stood straight up. He seemed much taller than before. "I think you're lying. Your friend doesn't have a secret. You couldn't tell me anything if you wanted to."

"Your secret isn't bad, so why does my friend's have to be?"

"Okay . . . I guess I can't argue with that." The neighbor crossed his hands behind his back and paced back and forth. "Can't be anything like my secret, so it must be something personal . . . maybe embarrassing. I know . . . he still wets his bed. He likes to play with dolls. He's an alien—"

Roy knew if he allowed the man to keep guessing, he might eventually figure out Nicholas' secret. He had to put a stop to this useless conversation. "I'll never tell, so you might as well drop it." Roy crossed his arms and puffed his chest out. "For someone who wants a secret kept, you sure don't—"

"Fine . . . fine . . . you're right. Maybe you can keep a secret," the man said. "But I'll be watching you. Don't forget, there are only two people in the world who know I can fly. I know I'm never going to tell. So that makes you the only source. I know your name and where you live. And it seems to me like you have a secret, too. I don't think your parents would think too kindly of you sneaking out and snooping on the neighbors. I would hate to have to pay them a visit."

"I guess we're even," Roy said with a half smirk.

"I guess we are." The man walked towards the middle of the living room. "C'mon in here and get comfortable. I tend to be long-winded."

CHAPTER 6

THE NEXT 8 MINUTES

The man pulled an overstuffed box from the corner and slid it to the center of the room. He patted the top of it. "Sit here."

"What's with all the boxes?" Roy asked, scooting his behind onto the lumpy surface, trying to sound genuinely interested and not nosey. "Are you moving somewhere?"

"As a matter of fact, I am moving in August," the man said.

"Looks like you could move tomorrow," Roy said. "Don't you have any furniture?"

"You're sitting down ... aren't you?"

"Well ... yeah ... I guess."

"So, what's the problem?" the man asked. "Besides, what's the most important feature of a chair—the fact that it looks like chair or the fact that you can sit on it?"

Roy had to admit the man had a point.

"Boxes are respectable surfaces for relieving one's legs," he continued, while pacing in front of Roy. "They are also ideal for storage and highly mobile. The contents of a box can redefine the function of the room in an instant." He wrapped his arms around a nearby box and let out a throaty grunt as he lifted it. "If I move this box of books into the room over there, it becomes a library. If I place my sleeping bag next to Shirley, then we are suddenly carrying on a conversation in my bedroom. Furniture limits how people use a space. I don't like being limited."

Roy wasn't sure how to respond, so he didn't.

The man dropped the box and stood directly in front of Roy. "Again, you are to tell no one. Anytime. Under any circumstance. I am only telling you more because you already know too much, and you might as well know everything instead of knowing just enough to get it all wrong."

"Definitely," Roy said.

The man extended his hand to Roy. "Hello, my name is Bartholemule Foot. You can call me Bart. I am a clothing fastener designer by day and an inventor by night. I used to work at Holden's Button Factory, right outside of town. It closed last month, and by summer's end, I will begin working at Joyner's Zipper Factory one state over. For now, I'm between jobs and finally have the time to test my Majestic Flyer."

Out of all the information presented, Roy honed in on one small detail. "Your last name is Foot?"

"Well," Bart said, unfazed by Roy's interruption, "it wasn't always Foot. My birth name is Tow—T-O-W—but everyone mistook it for T-O-E. You know—toe," he said, pointing to his foot.

"Yeah, I get it," Roy said. "But why's it Foot now?"

"You're a question guy. I like that. Most people stopped asking me questions a long time ago," Bart said. "I changed it to Foot because the toes extend from the foot, and since everyone assumed my last name was Toe, I thought I might as well change it to something more vital to the human body. People can lose a toe and it doesn't really matter." He began hopping on one foot. "But a foot . . . now that's a different story."

Roy watched his logically weird neighbor hop over to the large wall opposite the side door. He really liked the fact that Bart could make odd make more sense than ordinary. If Nicholas had changed his name for the same reason, Roy probably would've laughed or thought he'd gone completely crazy. If Nicholas' family lived out of boxes doubling as chairs, they would spend all their time at Roy's house. But even though he barely knew Bart, everything coming from his mouth seemed to make sense.

"You worked at a button factory?" Roy asked. "I didn't know there was a button factory in town."

"On yeah, it was there for years. I'm wearing some of their products right now." He pinched a button on his shirt and pulled it away from his chest. "You probably have some of their products in your closet too. I probably designed some of them." As he released the button, he stared straight ahead and spoke softly. "It was sad to see the factory close. I was lucky to get a job not too far away."

Roy didn't know his part of the country had so many factories that made fasteners for clothes. He never really gave much thought to buttons or zippers. "Did another button factory put it out of business?"

"Not exactly . . . they moved the factory to another country," he mumbled. Bart faced the wall. He pulled out a chunky writing pen from his pocket and began to write.

"Wait," Roy interrupted, once again. "Should you be doing that?" Bart looked confused. "Should you be writing on the wall? Isn't someone going to move into this house after you leave? Won't they be mad?"

Bart chuckled and looked back at Roy without moving his feet. "I keep forgetting that no one else knows of my many inventions. I guess I should explain. This is an Invisoscript," he began, weaving the device over and under his fingers like a baton. "It contains evaporatable ink. After about ten minutes, anything I have written with it will disappear without a trace—no matter what I write on."

Although he would give up at least a year's worth of allowance for one, Roy still asked, "What's the point in that? Why would you want what you've written to disappear?"

"Another great question," Bart pointed out, appearing to have much more patience for rude interruptions than the average adult. "You see, I invented evaporatable ink because I thought it would be useful to be able to jot down an idea or list or reminder anywhere. You wouldn't have to scramble to find a piece of paper. You could write without worrying about what you were writing on . . . take a mental picture, and it would be in your mind when you needed it."

To prove his point, Bart completely turned towards Roy and began scribbling random numbers and marks on his arm and pants. "I thought the Invisoscript would be a huge seller. That is, until I found out that less than one percent of the world's population has a photographic memory." In a satirical effort to see his forehead, he blindly wrote "1%" right above his faint eyebrows and continued to explain, "This statistic led me to the conclusion that most people wouldn't want what they had written to disappear after ten minutes."

As the marks began to fade, Bart turned back towards the wall. "It serves me well, though. I can sketch and formulate my inventions anywhere and know that no one will ever have access to my ideas."

"You have a photographic memory?" Roy asked. "I don't think I know anyone like that."

"Well . . . you do now," Bart said, twirling around and throwing his arms up as if he'd given an award-winning stage performance. In the seconds that followed, Roy and Bart shared their first laugh.

"You should be famous—like one of those people you see on the science channel."

"Nah, most people think my ideas are silly . . . or worthless . . . or impossible."

"Looks to me like you're proving everyone wrong," Roy said. "You can fly like a bird. Who else can say that?"

"Well, it's kind of hard to prove people wrong when

you don't want them to ever know you're right." Bart placed the end of the Invisoscript to the wall. "Do you want to hear about my flyer or not?"

CHAPTER 7

THE NEXT 1.75 HOURS

As Bart began to write, every cell in Roy's body seemed to wake up and take notice. Shirley lay down with her bottom facing the wall. Evidently, she'd heard it all before. Bart spoke and wrote simultaneously. The information spewed out of him like a crimped water hose yanked straight. To Roy, the knowledge emerging before him was just as beautiful and significant as any piece of art displayed in a museum—the numbers, their relationships, the sketches. In no time, Bart covered the wall with theories of body mechanics, wing design concepts, mechanical amplification formulas, and aerodynamic graphics. He explained that most bird-wing flying attempts failed because humans don't have the strength to maneuver the wings to produce enough thrust to gain the lift needed to fly.

"But, after 71,399.6 hours and 103 prototypes, I finally figured it out," Bart said, holding out one arm. "An elliptical wing shape works the best for holding up a human. And what better material to cover the wings than with actual bird feathers—a no brainer, if you ask me. Also, the flexible aluminum frame enables me to twist and fold the wings to control thrust and drag—just like a real bird." Bart moved his arm up and down. To Roy, it almost looked like he was treading water. "And, instead of being only attached to the arms, the wings are hinged on the back of the vest. That way, the wings move fluidly and magnify the power in my arms. The hinge design also allows for individual wing movement, so I can steer through the air. It's really quite simple . . . when you think about it."

"It took you 71,3—"

"399.6 hours to come to this conclusion—yes," Bart said. "I've been working on this since I was twelve."

Roy was speechless. Bart was about his age when he began pursuing his dream. Suddenly, being in the presence of such an accomplished individual wasn't doing much for Roy's self-esteem. To think, the only goal he had achieved was gaining access into Bart's house. Roy felt stupid, small, and useless. Bart was living proof that childhood had the potential to be much more than making plans and preparing for adulthood. At that moment, Roy decided he was tired of planning; it was time to do. And who better to learn from than Bart?

"I still don't understand why you wouldn't want to tell the whole world about all your hard work," Roy said. "You'd never have to work at a factory if you sold your ideas."

"What's wrong with working at a factory?" Bart asked. "If I hadn't worked at Holden's, I wouldn't have learned about plastic and how to mold it. Plus, they let me bring home all the unused plastic and scrap aluminum I wanted. And when they closed, I left with more stuff." Bart looked around the room as though most of his belongings had come from his former workplace. "Besides, there's nothing wrong with an honest day's work. How else would I have earned cash to support my inventions?"

"I didn't mean working at a factory was bad. But if you told everyone, you'd probably make a billion dollars, and then you could focus on flying . . . and your other inventions. Isn't that what you really want to do . . . all the time . . . invent?" Roy asked.

Bart stepped back from the wall with his back towards Roy. He stared straight ahead as though hypnotized by his own drawings. "Years ago, I did tell people about what I was working on—they all laughed and said it couldn't be done. 'It's a waste of time,' they would say. So, I stopped telling people. Besides, I didn't need the negative energy. You know?"

"Yeah, I guess I know what you mean," Roy said. "When I tell my mom about my ideas, she only looks at me and smiles. I can tell she hears what I'm saying, but I don't think she takes the time to understand what it all means to me."

"Oh, I'm sure she believes in you. She's your mom—it's her job," Bart replied, sounding, once again, like the typical adult. "Besides, I actually find it more exciting to keep my inventions a secret. It makes life more interesting when you know something other people don't. Come to think of it . . . I FEEL more interesting, and I'd much rather be interesting than boring."

Roy could definitely relate to the feeling of wanting to be interesting. When it came to picking sports teams, or making their party guest list, or selecting a partner for a school project, all the kids in his class acted as though he wasn't worth considering. It wasn't that no one liked him—everyone simply ignored him. Like the bowls of mushy pears in the lunch line only taken when all the ice cream and cookies were all gone. Sure, Nicholas liked hanging out with him, but he was only one kid out of at least 100 he knew. And even with Nicholas, Roy was usually the one doing all the compromising. He didn't like soccer nearly as much as his best friend did. He mostly ran up and down the field to make it look like he was participating. Nicholas was the star athlete, and Roy was his clumsy sidekick most kids at the park referred to as "what's-his-face." Roy bet Bart hadn't been good at soccer either—or popular—or the teacher's favorite. None of that seemed to matter now. Bart was doing exactly what he wanted.

Bart finished up by drawing the final part of the vest. "You see, I need to fly with my body parallel to the ground. So, I came up with the idea to extend the vest down on the sides for two leg channels." He tapped the side of his thighs. "That way, when I push off the roof at a ninety degree angle, I can propel my legs into the molded channels as I leap off the roof. And presto, my body is positioned just like a bird's."

"No wonder it took you 71—"

"399.6 hours and 103 prototypes . . . yeah . . . you have to have a lot of patience to be an inventor," Bart said. "Thomas Edison and his team invented a thousand ways the light bulb didn't work before they invented the one way to make it work. And we're all thankful they didn't give up." He looked up at the dusty light fixture above Roy's head.

Roy looked at the light. He knew the basic story about Edison and the light bulb, but never really thought about all the effort it took to make artificial light a reality. Light bulbs, buttons, zippers, no one really gave them much thought until they stopped working. Last month, Lisa Lambert interrupted his presentation to the class to let him know his fly was unzipped. That was about the only time, before tonight, Roy had thought about how zippers actually worked.

Bart stood at the opposite end of the wall and stared at Roy. Most of what he'd written had faded, or was fading, and the only legible part remaining was a small patch at the bottom, near his feet. Roy stared back. He needed to say something. He didn't want Bart to think he wasn't listening. "The feathers—where'd you get all the feathers?"

"Most of them come from the local aviary. I volunteer there from time to time, and they let me take all the feathers I want. I have been collecting them since—"

"Since you were twelve."

"Exactly—you are listening," Bart said with a grin.

Blurp . . . pop . . . hiss . . . spat.

"Not again." Bart took off into the kitchen. Roy and Shirley ran after him. They all stood around the stove as

Bart moved the gurgling pot to an unlit burner and stirred the contents.

"What's that?" Roy scrunched his nose.

"It's glirp."

Roy looked down into the giant pot of bubbling white goo with black swirls. "Okay, but what's glirp?"

"It's a recipe I'm working on for the Majestic Flyer."

"How does it work with the flyer? Wait . . . I know." Roy smirked. "It's glue that holds the feathers on."

"No . . . that's a pretty good guess, though. I actually don't glue the feathers on. It would weigh them down and clump them together. I have to thread the feathers on with nylon string—one by one."

"So what's it for?" Roy asked, sniffing the pot's contents.

"Well . . ." Bart started, as though he were preparing himself for another long speech, "it's great being able to soar like a bird. Even so, I want to do something good with my flyer. And since my BinGloculars help me see criminals at night, I'm going to turn my flying sessions into crime fighting missions. Might as well try and do something good for the town—if I can."

"BinGloculars?"

"Yea . . . BinGloculars," Bart said. "They're nothing but auto focusing binoculars I turned into goggles. They have night vision lenses, split down the middle so I can see normal at the top and ten times closer through the bottom." He curled his fingers towards his thumbs and brought them to his eyes. "They were actually one of my first inventions. I made them from parts and pieces I picked up from garage sales . . . and in the trash. I'm always amazed at what people throw away."

Roy looked at the man before him. It was hard to believe that someone so amazing could be amazed by other people's thoughtless actions. "So, if the glirp isn't glue—what is it?"

"Well, last week when I was flying around, I noticed some kids vandalizing the high school," Bart said. "It made me furious, and what's worse, I couldn't do anything about it. I was stuck, watching from the sky. I thought about swooping down and scaring them, but I was afraid I might hit some power lines. So, I circled above until they left."

"Did they see you?"

"No, they didn't even notice me," he said. "If I could have dropped something on them, then it would've scared them away. I didn't want to hurt them or anything. I only wanted to stop them."

Looking up from the pot, Roy grinned as if he'd just gotten the punch line to a joke he was told days earlier.

"Oh, I get it. This is a giant pot of bird turds. You're going to drop this goo on people—like how a bird poops."

"I guess that's one way of putting it," Bart stated while sticking a thermometer into the pot's contents. "Personally, I prefer glirp. It's more respectful to the birds."

"I guess," Roy said. "But it's only poop. They leave it everywhere—not much need for respect. They don't seem to care where it lands."

"They don't?" Bart cocked his head with a phony puzzled look on his face. "I wonder. I guess we all have different ways of seeing things. I like to think that bird poop has some sort of meaning or message. I believe they're very strategic with their placement. Think about it from a bird's point of view. All those splats to see from the sky—they probably make some kind of pattern or design. Or, maybe they represent some secret language or symbols birds use to communicate with one another. I don't think it's random at all . . . or gross, for that matter. I think the idea is mysterious and beautiful. Humans could learn a lot from birds. If we only tried."

"Huh, I guess I never looked at it that way," Roy said. "I guess I've been looking at a lot of things the wrong way."

"Not wrong," Bart said. "You see things the way you've been taught to see them . . . like everyone else." He lifted the pot and carried it over to the far counter. "I think it's ready." He scooped the wooden spoon out of the pot and catapulted its contents through the air. The glirp splatted onto the farthest kitchen wall like a bug hitting a speeding car's windshield. "See the consistency —not too runny or too thick. This recipe is the best yet." He opened the cabinet door above him and pulled out a rectangular, plastic container with a large, screw-on cone in the middle and hoses coming out either end.

Roy walked over to the blob of glirp clinging to the wall. He stuck his finger in it and turned to Bart. "What's this stuff made out of?"

"Oh, some paper, water, flour, honey, and black pepper," Bart replied. Roy was going to ask about the black pepper. However, he knew Bart had a good reason for adding it, so he didn't bother. Instead, Roy looked at the contraption in Bart's hands. "How does that thing work?"

"This invention here is the GlirpBlaster." He stretched out the contraption. "See these Velcro strips? They attach to the strips on the center of my vest and hold the dispenser in place. The tip is aimed towards the ground when I'm flying." Gripping the ends of the tubes, Bart extended his arms. "These tubes attach to handles on my wings. When I want to dispense some of the glirp, I simply squeeze the handles to force air down the tubes—and BLAST—glirp shoots out the tip and, hopefully, onto the person causing mischief. Brilliant. Right?" Bart asked without really expecting an answer.

"Are you kidding me? It's more than brilliant. It's genius—and funny—the best crime fighting tool I've ever heard of."

Bart stuck his hand in the cooling glirp and carefully lifted it back out. His shiny, white, black specked hand looked as though it was melting back down into the pot. "The great thing about the glirp is that it gets stickier and harder the longer it stays on something, making it difficult to wash off. It's the ideal material to slow a criminal down without hurting them, or anything else, if I were to miss."

"Yeah, and they'll probably think it's a giant bird turd . . . and that makes it much better," Roy said, wishing he had a GlirpBlaster to bomb the snooty, neighborhood girls. "You're like some kind of superhero —except you're better than a superhero because you're real. Plus, you're my neighbor."

"Well, I don't' know about being a superhero." Bart held back a grin.

Roy smiled. Suddenly, a frightening realization shot through his brain. Time—he'd totally lost track of the time. He brought his left wrist to his face. The sapphire numbers read 5:38 a.m. Only two minutes to get home.

CHAPTER 8

THE NEXT 15.5 HOURS

"I have to go. My dad will be waking up any minute," Roy announced. "I want to know more—everything. Can I come back tomorrow night?"

"I don't know about that." Bart raised an eyebrow. "I didn't think about the fact you had folks that might check on you and find you missing."

"They'll never know—trust me. They don't know I'm up every night." Roy smiled bigger than usual. "How could they? They're daylifers."

Bart looked down at Roy and crookedly smiled back. "Okay . . . yeah. But, I'm planning on flying tomorrow . . . if I can get the flyer ready."

"Can I come around one o'clock? Maybe I can help you. I can keep Shirley company while you fly . . . so she won't bark," Roy offered, hoping to convince Bart his presence would be useful.

"Fine—one o'clock—don't get caught."

"Never," Roy assured him as he headed towards the side door.

Bart called out behind him, "You won't tell anyone, right? I mean no one."

Roy turned around smiling. "No way. Your secret will go with me to my grave . . . if that's what you want."

"To your grave, then."

"To my grave."

Now, all Roy had to do was get back to his bedroom without getting caught. He slithered along the fence, staying well within its shadow's edge. He spotted a few cars passing by his house and knew the risk of exposure would be high. He shot out between the houses, checked each way for any sign of headlights, and took off towards his window. He reached the darkness engulfing the oak tree and grabbed the fire escape. He hugged the rope like a secret agent dangling above a tank of hungry piranhas. His hands were sweaty, and the climb took twice as long as it should've. Finally, he tumbled through the window, landing with a thud, half on the chest below his window and half on the hard, wooden floor. He tucked the rope out of sight, between two branches, closed the sash and scrambled under his covers.

He did it. That's all he could think. HE DID IT. He couldn't believe it. The night had turned out better than he had ever imagined. He couldn't help but think about what he would've missed had he chickened out and gone home. He'd made a new friend—maybe a new best friend. Bart was a lot like him, except for the age difference, which didn't bother Roy, although he couldn't say the same for Bart. He wasn't sure how his new friend felt about him. All he knew was that trust was issue number one.

Still, Roy wanted to be more than a trustworthy sponge soaking up everything that oozed out of Bart. He had to prove he could be useful too. If not, his new friend would probably get tired of him and shoo him home. If Roy wanted to hang out at a superhero's house every night, then he was going to have to justify his presence.

Click . . . squeak. Roy's door opened and a wedge of light cut across his bed. Roy squeezed his eyes shut. He was sure it was his dad checking on him, wondering what that loud thud was. Even after he heard the door latch shut, he kept his eyes closed until his dad's footsteps headed down the stairs.

Knowing he was officially safe, Roy opened his eyes

and returned to his thoughts. He knew exactly what he could do for Bart. Something he knew Bart would never do for himself. He would make up a superhero name for his new friend. Bart definitely needed one, and Roy was the ideal person to fulfill the task.

Most of the superheroes he knew of had names ending with "man" like Superman, Spiderman, or Batman. But Bart was a different kind of superhero. He didn't have special powers he was born with or acquired through a freak accident. He invented his powers out of practically nothing, so the name had to be equally impressive.

Roy had a few ideas: The Turdinator, Glirpoman, and The Flying Glirper. All pathetic, he thought. Convinced sleep deprivation was preventing the ideal name from emerging, he attempted to get some rest.

Roy gave a slight jerk as a voice startled him into consciousness. "Wake up, sleeping beauty." It was Melonie poking his face.

"Get outta here!" Roy slapped Melonie's hand away. "You're not supposed to be in my room."

"Mom said to 'GET UP.' We have errands to run," Melonie insisted, then turned and skipped back down the hall. Errands with Mom—ugh. He would rather scrub toilets all day. Moanfully, Roy peeled himself out of bed. Days like today reminded him of why he adored the nights; no one ever ran errands at 2:00 in the morning. There was nothing worse than a Monday at the grocery store and other horribly boring, mom-like places.

He only made it through the grueling morning hours by thinking of the darkness to come.

He was relieved when his mom checked off the last place on her list around noon. He was looking forward to a quick lunch at home followed by quiet time in his room.

But Roy should have known that Melonie had her own agenda.

Just when he thought they were heading to the house, his demanding, opinionated, spoiled little sister pulled out her own list—and it was much longer than his mom's and much more embarrassing. Unlike Roy, lists came easy to Melonie because she knew exactly what she wanted and how to get it. If only he could be more like her, he wouldn't be wasting his day running errands.

Roy managed to wait outside the jewelry store while

Melonie and his mom exchanged a bracelet. Later on, he hid between the clothes racks as the two shopped for bathing suits for the upcoming trip. But when they pulled up to the doll store, Roy just about lost it and refused to get out of the car.

"Roy, it's too hot for you to stay out here." His mom looked around the parking lot. "Plus, it doesn't look very safe. C'mon . . . we'll only be a minute."

Of course, Melonie had to make the situation worse. "They have boy dolls. There's one in the catalogue that looks just like you."

"C'mon, Roy." They both stood by the open car door and stared at him. Roy let out the loudest grumble of his life and followed them into the store. Melonie dragged her mom to the counter to pick up a doll that had been back-ordered since Christmas. Roy stayed at the front, right next to the window display of a doll family that appeared to be enjoying their miniature kitchen, bedroom, and living room sets. The doll's blank eyes made them look like zombies that had taken over someone else's home. The only interesting thing about the whole setup was the little stuffed dog sitting next to his bowl in the kitchen.

Roy looked around the rest of the store. No one, including his sister and mom, seemed to care that he was there. So, he decided to squeeze some amusement out of an otherwise horrible day by transforming the window display into something worth talking about. He finished right before Melonie rushed to him to show off her doll. His mom was right behind her, and Roy followed them out the door. As they walked towards the car, Roy turned around to admire his work. Much better, he thought. All stuffed dogs should be allowed to eat dinner in bed while little girl dolls eat off the floor.

He wondered how long it would take anyone to notice.

Once at home, Roy rushed upstairs to his room. Ideas for Bart's superhero name had been flashing in and out of his brain all day, but now that he finally had a chance to write them down, he couldn't remember any of them. Even after the monotonous day of nothingness finally ended with the rest of the Winklesteens heading off to bed, his list of names wasn't looking any better.

1. The Flying Turdinator

2. Winged Glirpoman

Why were ideas so cruel? One minute they're yelling in your ear, and the next minute, they're nothing but a faint ringing, taunting you with the greatness that could've been. If he only had an Invisoscript and a photographic memory, he would never be faced with this dilemma.

Though he was off to a slow start, Roy knew Bart's superhero name (he only needed one) lingered somewhere in the depths of his exhausted mind. Sleep— that's all it would take for the best idea to reveal itself. He set his alarm for midnight and decided to work on the list before he headed to Bart's house.

CHAPTER 9

THE NEXT 5.5 HOURS

Roy sat straight up when his alarm sounded. He slammed his hand down on the top of the clock and fumbled for the off switch. For a moment, he'd forgotten why he had set it. Confused and a little shaky, he tiptoed to his door and cracked it open. He was certain another Winklesteen had heard the bellowing beeps.

The hall was dark and dead quiet. It's just paranoia, he thought, and rightfully so. Sneaking out of the house was a big deal, and Bart's secret was an even bigger deal. No one could ever know that he and the secretive neighbor were friends—it would raise too much suspicion. The greatest summer of his life, his parents' trust, and Bart's friendship all rested on his shoulders. No problem, he reassured himself. He just had to stay calm and cool.

Before he turned on his desk lamp, he peered out his window towards Bart's house. The attic light was on. He knew Bart was working on the Majestic Flyer. Roy hoped that soon he would be in that attic, too. Like his mission last night was to get a closer look at his neighbor, Roy had a mission tonight—to see the Majestic Flyer up close.

He flicked on his lamp and stared at the pitiful list of superhero names. He knew the name had to be mysterious, powerful, and, of course, about flying. Like he had anticipated, sleep proved to be highly beneficial, and an idea sprung out of his head like a jack-in-the-box:

1. The Flying Turdinator
2. Winged Glirpoman
3. The Soaring Phantom (Fantom?)

It wasn't a long list, but it was enough. And it was Roy's first attempt at proving to Bart that he could be useful.

His desk clock read 12:21 a.m. Roy folded the list and started to put it in his pocket, only to realize his typical summer attire of a t-shirt and elastic band shorts didn't offer one. Buzzing with confidence, he knew exactly how to fix the problem. Roy felt full of brilliant ideas and knew his time with Bart had to be the reason. He decided to put on a button down shirt and a pair of jeans. He rummaged through his closet until he found the ideal ensemble. As he put on his shirt, he examined its round blue buttons. He wondered if Bart would notice them. His jeans were hot and stiff, but they had a zipper, and he hoped Bart would appreciate the thought. After securing the Ooberleeben around his wrist, Roy was ready to put Mission Majestic Flyer into action.

12.57 a.m. finally made its way onto the Ooberleeben display, and Roy headed towards the fire escape. Lacking the smooth moves of a seasoned spy, he bumped his dresser with his elbow while opening the window. The whole thing wobbled, sending his soccer ball tumbling to the hardwood floor and bouncing three times before rolling into his closet door.

For a few minutes, Roy stood absolutely still, listening for any signs of an awakened family member.

All remained quiet. He squatted on the windowsill and grabbed the end of the fire escape. He tugged until it fell free towards the ground.

Squueeeakkk.

Busted! Roy thought, as that sound could only mean one thing—someone had opened his bedroom door.

"Roy . . . the monsters are gonna get me," Melonie said, as she stood in the doorway rubbing her eyes.

Relieved, Roy whirled around and rushed over to her.

"No, there aren't any monsters. My soccer ball fell off the dresser and made a loud noise," he said, as he put both hands on her shoulders and turned her around back towards the hall. "You need to get back in bed. C'mon, I'll tuck you in."

"But you're not in bed," Melonie noted, now more awake. "What were you doing out your window?"

"I—I was shooing a moth out of my room. It was bothering me." Proud of his clever response, Roy guided Melonie back to her bed and tucked her tightly under the poufy covers. "Here's your doll. Close your eyes and go to sleep."

"But . . . the monsters," Melonie said as she lifted her head off her pillow.

"I told you, it was my soccer ball that made those noises. Besides, even if there were monsters, which there are not, you know I'd never let them get you." Roy knelt down next to her bed. "I'll stay with you till you fall asleep." Melonie pulled her doll into her chest and smiled. She placed her small, soft hand on top of his and closed her eyes. Roy didn't move a muscle. Whatever he needed to do to get to her to fall asleep was fine with him.

On the way back down the hall to his room, he

considered the possibility of Melonie being a nightlifer like him. What if it runs in the family? Nights would never be the same if he had to share them with his little sister. Unwilling to accept the most minuscule chance of that ever happening, Roy erased the thought from his mind and returned to his room.

Back at his window, Roy slid down the fire escape without a sound. He tore across the street, in between the houses, and up to Bart's side door. He knocked lightly. When there was no answer, Roy figured Bart probably couldn't hear him from the attic. So, he knocked again—louder and longer. Still nothing.

He knew he couldn't keep knocking. Even if Bart couldn't hear, his neighbors probably could. He stared at the faded, brass knob. Maybe Bart had unlocked it for him since he knew he would be in the attic and unable to hear anything. Roy placed his hand on the cool metal and slowly began to turn. His wrist twisted all the way over to the right. He pushed the door in a little and peeked through the gap. His heart was pounding much more than last night. But unlike the pounding your heart does when the teacher calls on you for an answer you don't know, this was good pounding. He continued to open the door enough to poke his head inside. The moon provided a hint of light for him to see the box he'd sat on the night before. He hesitated for a second.

Reminding himself that no risk meant no reward, Roy decided to go for it. He crept all the way inside and shut the door. Roy stared at the wall once covered with Bart's formulas and drawings. Only Bart and Roy knew what had been there. The new owners of the house would never know the formula for one of the greatest inventions was right in front of them.

Like he thought, Bart and Shirley weren't downstairs. Last night, he had barely noticed the stairs at the end of the living room. Tonight, they were almost all he noticed. If he wanted his mission to proceed as planned, climbing them was the next step.

He pressed his feet against the edge of the first step. His eyes followed the jagged, ascending pattern up the wall until it completely faded into darkness.

"B-Bart," Roy tried to call out loudly. "Bart ... Shirley? Anyone there?" There was no reply. Roy had no choice. As his feet felt their way up each stair tread, his clammy hand slid along the wooden railing. When he reached the top, the moonlight eerily revealed a long hall with a hint of light coming from a doorway on the far right side. He sprinted towards the inviting glow and passed through the doorway where a folding staircase, stretched wide open, startled him into a skidding stop. He knew exactly where the steps led.

He negotiated the rickety stairs until half his body emerged through the opening. Finally, he had made it to Bart's attic.

The room was much different than he had envisioned. There were no bubbling beakers or spiral hoses with wisps of steam sporadically escaping release valves or energy containment chambers humming in each of the corners. Instead, the vast, stuffy space had nothing more than stacks of boxes, a row of large gray buckets against the wall, and a few folding tables covered with supplies found in the average garage. The only unusual things in Bart's attic were all the feathers stuck to the unfinished walls and tumbling across the floor. Then there was Bart, standing at a table with the large pot of glirp from the night before.

Bawoof . . . bawoof. At Shirley's bark, Bart swung around so quickly that the pot of glirp flew out of his hands. A wavy, liquid cloud filled the air above Bart and Shirley, then flopped down on top of them like a wet bed sheet. Covered in glirp, Bart attempted to step towards Roy, only to slip on the slimy floor, which flung his legs clear above his head—SPLAT. Bart's behind hit the floor square on, splashing Shirley with more glirp.

Bart scooped the glirp away from his eyes.

"Roy . . . when did you get here?"

"Are you okay?" Roy asked as he scurried up the rest of the stairs and over to Bart. "I knocked and called your name, but there was no answer. I didn't mean to scare you or Shirley, but you said one o'clock, and I thought you'd be expecting me. I didn't know what to do—the door was unlocked. I—"

"Yeah, you're right, we did agree to one o'clock," Bart said, as he assessed the mess around him. Roy grabbed Bart's arm and helped him to his feet. "What a disaster," he said, shaking the excess glirp off his arms.

Roy began scraping the glirp off Bart. He couldn't believe what a catastrophe he'd caused. "I'll help you clean it up. I'm sorry. I didn't—"

"Yea . . . well . . . glirp happens . . . doesn't it?" Bart pushed Roy's hands away. "It's no big deal. I'll get over it. At least now, when I glirp someone, I'll know how they feel. Trust me . . . it's no fun." Bart faked a smile. "I'm convinced, more than ever, that glirp is the ideal crime stopping solution. Grab some of those rags over there . . . would you?"

Roy reached for the towels, handed one to Bart, and began helping him wipe off. He could sense Bart's frustration. He knew his neighbor was looking at him and the mess and wondering why he had ever let a kid into his life. Roy felt panicky. He didn't know what to say.

Bart pushed Roy's hands away again, "Why don't you tend to Shirley. I can manage." Roy cleaned Shirley, the floor, and the wall as best he could. The more he tried rubbing the glirp off Shirley, the stickier and more matted her fur became.

Roy had to say something. "I can't believe the mess I made. I really am sorry. Is there any way I can make it better?"

"Yea . . . next time, don't be so sneaky . . . at least when you're around me." Bart's mood seemed to lighten. "Shirley, I guess now is as good a time as any for a quick shower. Let's go."

While Bart and Shirley rinsed off, Roy got a chance to wander around the mysterious attic. On the wall behind the stair opening hung the Majestic Flyer. Below it, several individual wings were propped against the wall. Even from across the attic, Roy could make out the rigid contour of the black, plastic vest. Framed against the plush curves of each wing, it seemed to grunt manliness.

Roy walked over to the flyer. He ran his hand down the length of the left wing. Beneath the airy layer of feathers, his fingers traced the delicate aluminum frame.

What a masterpiece, he thought. It should be hanging in the Smithsonian Museum, like all the other historical flying machines. No doubt, Roy knew it would be the main attraction. As much as the world needed to know about Bart's accomplishment, he would keep it to himself. This wasn't his secret to tell.

All dressed in tight, black clothing, Bart, with Shirley resting across his neck and shoulders like a scarf, entered the attic. "I think I have enough glirp to make a test run tonight. Here, why don't you help me," Bart said, while handing the GlirpBlaster to Roy. "Hold this." Roy held the blaster steady while Bart poured in the gooey concoction. "Ah, the 571AX—that's a great button," Bart noted as he placed the pot of glirp back on the table.

"Did you design these?" Roy asked.

"No, those aren't mine, but that's okay. It's still a great design. Wear them proudly," Bart said with a grin. Roy looked down at his buttons. If his friend could take pride in something so small and seemingly insignificant, so could he.

Bart opened the attic window and poked his head out. "Well, I think everything is about ready to go." He licked his finger and held it in front of his face. "Hardly any wind. Should be a great night to fly."

Bart retrieved a very old-looking helmet, like some of the first football players used to wear, and secured it around his chin. He picked up the BinGloculars from a nearby table and positioned them so they sat on top of his head. "Grab the GlirpBlaster for me. You're going to have to hand it to me after I get on the roof." Roy nodded with a smile. Bart slid a ladder underneath the hatch door. "Guess it's a good thing you're here . . . not sure I could do this on my own," Bart said with a wink. Roy was happy to hear his friend needed his help.

"Okay, here we go," Bart said. "After I get on the roof, climb up the ladder and hand me the blaster." He lifted the flyer off the wall hooks and folded the wings on top of one another like a book. The entire thing was so light, Bart dangled it over one shoulder like a jacket. He opened the hatch and made his way onto the roof. Roy cradled the GlirpBlaster and headed up the ladder after Bart.

As Roy poked his head out of the hatch opening, he felt his legs begin to tingle. Bart's roof was at least 10 times higher than it seemed from the ground. He realized his new friend was much braver than he had thought. Some people might consider Bart foolish, or crazy. Even so, a person who had the nerve to leap off a three-story roof with a homemade pair of wings could never be afraid of heights.

Roy wished he weren't afraid of heights.

Bart closed the vest around his body. He took the blaster from Roy and pushed it in place. He ran the tubing through the wing loops and forced the ends into a hole on the handle. He threaded his arms through the wing straps and gave the handles a tender squeeze. A stream of glirp gushed from the tip. Bart and Roy exchanged excited smiles. It was time to fly.

"Shut the hatch, and then I'll go. You can watch from the window," Bart said. "See ya in a little while."

"I'll be here . . . with Shirley," Roy said. Right after Roy lowered the hatch and started back down the ladder, he remembered the list in his pocket. There was no point in pulling it out now. It would have to wait until Bart returned.

Roy hustled to the attic window and watched for Bart to appear. His excitement alerted Shirley, and she followed behind him, jumping up on two legs and resting her paws on the windowsill. Not long after, they both heard Bart's footsteps making their way down the roof ridge. A few seconds later, Bart was soaring away from them.

Roy and Shirley sat down below the attic window and waited. Although the two of them didn't meet under the best of circumstances, Roy felt Shirley was really warming up to him. He rubbed her head gently to get a closer look at her ear. He wished Shirley could tell him how it got that way. She probably had quite a story. He would have to remember to ask Bart later.

The Ooberleeben glowed 2:28 a.m. The next few minutes felt like hours, and the next hour felt like days. By 3:30 a.m., Roy began to get anxious. Waiting for Bart to return was worse than waiting in a mile-long line to ride the highest roller coaster at the park. The anticipation made him want to burst. Occasionally, Roy and Shirley would look out the window and scan the sky for any signs of Bart. By 4:48 a.m., Roy was beginning to get concerned. As far as he knew, Bart's flights had never been this long. Roy was hoping the GlirpBlaster was such a success that Bart needed longer to prevent all the crime.

However, by 5:23 a.m., Roy was chewing on his favorite nail. His mind clogged with reasons as to why Bart hadn't returned. He may have crashed and could be hurt, or worse, unconscious. Maybe he'd hit his head and had amnesia. Maybe he was DEAD. Roy didn't have time to think anymore. It was time to do.

Desperate, he made his way downstairs, leaving Shirley whimpering at the attic opening. He ran out the side door and searched the entire sky. The vast blackness revealed nothing but a few faint stars and some passing clouds.

Out of nowhere, a car whizzed by. Roy ducked behind a bush before the headlights gave him away. The daylifers were waking up. He looked back towards his house. His parents' bedroom windows were dark, for the moment.

He didn't know what to do. The Ooberleeben seemed to yell 5:34 a.m. He knew he couldn't leave Shirley in the attic all by herself, so he made his way back up to the attic stairs. Her high-pitched bark said it all; she was worried about Bart, too.

Roy looked up at the agitated dog. "C'mon Shirley." He whistled and patted one of the stairs. Shirley circled around the opening. Clearly, she depended on Bart to get out of the attic. Shirley was a big dog, and Roy was a small guy. He climbed up to Shirley and stroked her head. He tried wrapping his arms around the lanky dog, but she was way too big. Roy grabbed Shirley's collar and began pulling and guiding her down the stairs one paw at a time. She was hesitant, but, eventually, they made it down together.

As much as Roy wanted to stay behind and comfort the frightened dog, it was time to get home. He wanted to leave Bart a note, but the only writing utensil available was a lone Invisoscript. Roy gave Shirley one more reassuring pat on the head and went out the side door. As he ran towards his house, he looked up in every direction. He could see nothing but empty sky for miles. Where could Bart possibly be?

Roy heard his father's footsteps in the hall shortly after he crawled into bed. Sure, he was safe. As for his friend, things weren't looking so good. Maybe he should tell his father. But what would he tell him? Even if his father believed his story, Roy wouldn't know where to look for Bart. He'd probably traveled miles away from the neighborhood. Besides, telling anyone would reveal Bart's secret. Something Roy promised he would never do, no matter what happened.

For now, Roy would have to wait until it was safe to return to Bart's house. Hopefully, his friend would be there, safe and sound, with some incredible story to tell. Hopefully.

CHAPTER 10

TIME? WHO CARES?

Roy didn't sleep. He couldn't. About every five minutes, he would look out his window for any signs his friend had returned. The attic was still lit up, meaning Bart had not returned to switch anything off. Somehow, he had to risk getting to Bart's during the day, and since he couldn't sleep, he had plenty of time to come up with a plan.

During breakfast, he told his mom he was going to fly his kite at the park. He assured her he would probably meet up with Nicholas and he might be gone all day. His mom didn't mind—she and Melonie had their own plans. They all finished up and headed out at the same time.

Roy ran out the door with his kite. He started down the street towards Nicholas' house and waited, out of sight, until he saw his mom and Melonie disappear down the street in the family car. He made it to Bart's in record speed. When he reached the side door, he knocked, then pounded, and called out Bart's name. He heard Shirley wailing and scratching on the other side, but Bart never answered.

When he opened the door, Shirley leapt on top of him and pinned him up against the wall with her paws. She looked directly into his dark, brown eyes and gave him a sloppy lick across the face.

"Bart? Are you here . . . are you okay?" Roy climbed up both sets of stairs and poked his head into the attic. Everything was exactly as he'd left it. He slumped down on the bottom attic stair and wrapped his arm around Shirley. It was now clearer than ever—Bart was most likely in trouble. He had to tell someone. Even if he didn't have a clue where Bart was, he could tell everything he knew to the police, his dad, and anyone else who was willing to help him search for his friend. Roy promised Bart he would never tell, but maybe Bart hadn't considered a situation like this. Maybe Bart was barely clinging to life and wanted him to tell someone before it was too late. Time to call the police. He would have to deal with his parents' anger and disappointment later.

"C'mon Shirley, let's go to my house." Roy grabbed

her wide collar and led her down to the side door. As he put his hand on the knob, he thought about what he was going to tell the police. What if they didn't believe him and refused to help him search for Bart?

Shwaamp! The door swung open and thumped Roy's forehead, knocking him back onto Shirley and onto the floor. There stood Bart with a surprised look on his face. "Whoa . . . kid . . . sorry . . . didn't know you were there." He helped Roy to his feet. "What are you doing here?"

"Bart! Where have you been? I—I was so worried. I was about to call the police. I didn't know what to do," Roy said, giving Bart a tight squeeze around his waist.

"I'm fine kid—glad I got home when I did. Sure don't want you calling the police about me."

"I didn't know what else to do. I couldn't leave you out there somewhere and not try to help you," Roy said, not letting go of Bart.

"Yeah, I guess . . . you're right. I never really considered the fact I had someone back here waiting for me." He grabbed Roy's arms and unwound them from his waist.

"I mean . . . I never have before. Sorry, kid. I'm just used to being on my own. You know . . . no one to answer to, no worrying about somebody worrying about me. You need to get home now. Your parents must be worried sick."

"No, it's okay," Roy assured him. "I went home—then came back, hoping you would be here. My parents don't know anything . . . no one does."

"Good. You're a good kid, Roy Winklesteen," Bart said, as he rustled Roy's hair.

"What happened?" Roy asked. "Where have you been? Where's the Flyer?"

"Uh . . . it's okay." Bart headed towards the kitchen. "I've got it hidden. I'll have to go pick it up tonight."

"Pick it up? Why'd you leave it?"

"I had to. I lost my train of thought fiddling with the GlirpBlaster," he began. "I clipped a tree branch and had to make a crash landing. Luckily, I landed in a field with an abandoned barn. I left the flyer inside it."

Roy couldn't believe how calm Bart was about the whole incident. Had he worried for nothing?

"It's happened before," Bart continued. "Well, not clipping trees, but the crash landing part. It comes with flying like a bird."

"Yeah, I guess," Roy replied, faking a smile. "But when did you crash? Why did it take so long for you to get back?"

"It happened pretty early on in my flight—south of town. I decided to wait until morning to head home.

Didn't want to make anyone suspicious." Bart leaned over the kitchen sink and splashed his face with some cold water. "It's really no big deal and nothing for you to worry about. I am fine . . . see." He dried his face and did a 360 turn. "I'm fine."

Roy watched his new friend pour a bowl of cereal as if he didn't have a care in the world. How could a grown man forget that he had left a kid in his attic? "I thought you were dead," Roy mumbled, looking down at the floor.

"Me . . . die? Not a chance, I am way too stubborn for that," Bart said, rummaging around for a spoon. "I know what to do if things don't go right. Trust me . . . I've had to get myself out of worse situations than last night. Nothing bad is going to happen. I promise."

Roy rubbed Shirley's ear and stared into her sad, brown eyes. She seemed to understand how silly Bart sounded. How could he make such a ridiculous promise? He flew off his roof every night with a set of wings he'd made from stuff no one else wanted. Even astronauts took less risk than he did.

"Shirley was shaking and upset. Maybe you forgot about me, but what about her? I had to help her down from the attic."

"Hey . . . yeah . . . thanks for doing that, kid. She

really seems to like you."

"I'm sure she likes you more and would be really sad if anything ever happened to you."

"I told you, I'm fine." Bart tossed the empty plastic cereal bowl in the sink. "The last thing I need is someone worrying about me."

"Sure. If you say so," Roy said, turning towards the side door. He didn't know what to think of Bart. But it was now clear to him that the only person Bart ever thought about was himself. Bart wasn't his friend. He wasn't anyone's friend—he didn't even care about Shirley. He just wanted to make sure his secret was safe, which was the only reason this conversation was even taking place.

Roy headed out the door. He flinched as the sunlight crashed into his eyes. He felt something tap his arm.

"You forgot your kite." Bart handed him the crumpled bundle of nylon fabric.

Roy turned around and grabbed it without looking up at Bart. "Thanks."

Bart put his hand on Roy's shoulder and turned him back around so their eyes met. "Hey . . . what if I come up with a solution so you never have to worry about me again?"

Roy nodded.

"I'll have something ready for tonight," Bart said. "For now, you need to get on home and get some rest. I need my assistant to be sharp."

Roy smiled a little. He didn't doubt Bart's ability to come up with a solution. What he doubted was Bart's ability to understand the problem. All Roy could do was wait and see. He grabbed Bart's extended hand and gave it a couple of tugs.

"Deal." They simultaneously agreed.

"Now . . . get outta here," Bart said.

Roy headed home with a racing mind and an exhausted body. He was relieved to have the Winklesteen place all to himself. He curled up on the tufted den couch and let out an exaggerated sigh. Bart was safe, so was his secret, and so was their friendship. There was nothing left for Roy to do but sleep.

CHAPTER 11

THE NEXT 12.5 HOURS

A tickling on his face startled Roy from his drooling nap. Once again, it was Melonie annoying him. This time, she was using her doll's stringy hair to stroke his face. "Roy . . . you sick or something?"

"No, can't I lie down without you bothering me?" Roy pushed the doll out of his face.

"Roy, is that you?" his mom asked, bending over the couch. "I didn't know you were home. Did you have fun with Nicholas?

"Yeah," he replied quickly.

She leaned closer and stroked his hair. "How'd your kite work out?"

"Okay . . . it's kinda flimsy." He stood up and didn't dare look his mom in the eyes. "I'm just tired from being at the park all day."

"Dinner will be ready in a little while. Go get cleaned up," she said as she returned to the kitchen.

Roy ran to his room. He felt like he'd taken a soccer ball right in the gut. This was the first time he had ever really lied to his mom. Sure, he had told little fibs before, like saying he'd brushed his teeth when he hadn't for at least a couple of days, or letting Melonie take the blame for eating all the cookies he'd devoured earlier that day. But this was his first BIG lie. What if his mom asked Nicholas about their kite-flying day in the park? Nicholas wouldn't know what she was talking about. For the first time, his nighttime activities were starting to complicate his daytime life. Lying was never part of his plan, and he had to put an end to it before the situation got out of hand. He couldn't risk losing his parents' trust.

Oddly, sneaking out of the house in the middle of the night didn't affect his stomach at all. When it came to spending time at Bart's, Roy found it easy to defend his actions. Bart was a genius, so he was bound to learn much more from him than any perky camp counselor. Plus, his parents were always telling him he should make more friends. Besides, if he didn't tell his parents anything, he wasn't lying.

By keeping everyone laughing at dinner, Roy

managed to prevent any more discussions about the day's activities. He knew that the book of jokes he'd bought at the book fair would eventually come in handy. Everything had worked out, and Roy's summer was back on track.

That is, until his dad had to go and complicate everything.

"So, Roy, we never have gotten an opportunity to talk about your list of summer adventures." For someone who had just heard some of the greatest jokes ever written, his dad seemed way too serious. "Why don't you go get it so we can talk about it?"

"I lost it."

"It didn't look very long. Why don't you try to remember what you wrote? You should remember—it seemed awfully important to you at the time," his dad replied.

"It's not important. It was really stupid. I don't care what we do this summer," Roy sharply stated as he dumped his plate into the sink. "We can go to Uncle Bill's and swim with the dolphins. That actually sounds fun . . . now that I've had time to think about it."

"I didn't think it was stupid," his dad persisted.

"Yeah, it was kinda stupid, Daddy," Melonie chimed in. "Don't you remember? Roy wanted us to swim with sharks. I want to go to Uncle Bill's house. Let's forget about Roy's dumb list."

"Well . . . Roy . . . it's up to you. Your mom and I are willing to talk about curing the Winklesteen family of our boring life."

Roy wanted to roll his eyes so badly, but he didn't. "Uh, we're not that boring. Can we just forget about it?"

"That's fine, honey," his mom said. "Uncle Bill's it is. He'll be happy to see us."

"Okay, I guess we'll forget it," his dad said, even though his eyes couldn't have agreed less.

After his dad's look of distrust, Roy knew spending the evening hiding in his room would only make things worse. So, he joined the family in the den to watch a show about the Grand Canyon. The hair-raising, bird's eye flyovers off the cliffs awed all the Winklesteens. For Roy, it made him want to fly that much more. Everything Roy saw, heard, smelled, and even tasted somehow made him think of Bart and the flyer, so he was more than pleased when the rest of the family decided to make an early night of it. For good measure, he let his parents tuck him in. Roy was hoping the extra "good son" effort would eliminate any trace notions of suspicion his dad still had.

Later that night, Roy dug his list of superhero names

out of his jeans now jammed in the laundry hamper. He headed over to Bart's the usual way at the usual time. Bart didn't answer his door, so Roy didn't hesitate to let himself in. He made lots of commotion climbing the stairs, as he wasn't about to cause another disaster. Like Bart promised, he presented Roy with the perfect gadget to prevent any possibility for further miscommunication between the two friends.

"See, this is your piece," Bart showed Roy as he placed a sleek headphone set on Roy's head and positioned the slim microphone close to his mouth. "You turn the switch on right here, on this ear piece. When I put my headphones on, we can talk to each other. The system should have about a six-mile range. Why don't you run downstairs and we'll test it."

Roy didn't waste a second. He made it down to the box in the middle of the living room and switched on the earpiece.

"Testing . . . testing. Bart, come in, Bart."

"I hear you loud and clear, mission control," Bart responded. "I think we're ready for GlirpBlaster mission number two." Roy headed back to the attic excited that he was in charge of mission control and that he would be in touch with Bart throughout his entire flight.

Bart suited up, grabbed the flyer, and climbed the

ladder to the hatch. Once again, Roy handed him the GlirpBlaster, and then he and Shirley waited at the window. Bart's voice came in loud and clear, "I'm off, into the sky to wipe out crime from way up high!"

Thump, thump, thump, thump . . . shwoop. Roy and Shirley watched as Bart soared over the neighborhood and out of sight. Roy knew now, more than ever, Bart had to have a superhero name. No one that flew like a bird and blasted criminals with glirp should be called "Bartholemule Foot."

Roy bent the microphone close to his mouth. "Bart, come in Bart. This is mission control."

"I hear you mission control," Bart replied, his voice was faint and crackly. "Just soaring over downtown—on my way to the high school."

"Keep me posted on what you see."

"Will do."

Roy sat patiently and listened. He didn't want to bother Bart and cause an accident. The Ooberleeben read 2:54 a.m.

Suddenly, Bart's crackling voice exclaimed, "Over the graveyard, I see something, some people—going to circle and pass over again."

Roy jumped up and looked out the window. Shirley followed. "I hear you."

"It's a few people. I think they are painting on the gravestones—time to put the GlirpBlaster to the test."

"Get 'em, Bart," Roy said. He pressed the earphone closer to his ear, but he couldn't make out what was going on.

"Take that," Bart stated with bold determination. "YES. I got two of them. Coming home—can't afford to be spotted."

"See ya soon." Roy and Shirley waited at the window. Roy was glad Bart's mission was shorter than usual. He couldn't wait to connect the crucial events with the abundance of details his friend was sure to provide. Within minutes, Bart was flying directly towards the attic window. The view was quite an impressive sight. He didn't look like a man wearing a vest with wings. Instead, he looked like a man born to fly—in complete control—powerful—regal—like he was king of the sky.

Bart soared right above the window and *thump, thump, thump, thump,* onto the roof. It sounded like a smooth landing. He opened the hatch and lowered the flyer through the hole. Roy helped as much as he could.

Bart had a huge grin on his face. "Mission accomplished!"

"I want to hear everything. Did the GlirpBlaster work like you thought? Did the people see you? Did—"

"Hang on, kid. Give me a second," Bart said. He secured the flyer on the wall hooks and removed the rest of his equipment. Everything seemed to have a specific resting place, even if it was nothing more than a clear spot on a folding table.

Finally, the two friends sat on the floor across from one another.

Bart confirmed that it wasn't long into his flight when he had noticed movement in the graveyard behind the old stone church. He had circled high and used his BinGloculars to hone in on the activity. When he had determined the trespassers were vandals, he'd instinctually gone into crime fighting mode. "I knew it was the ultimate opportunity to engage the GlirpBlaster. So, I went for it. I circled as low as I could without being seen and put my glirp dispensing calculations to the test." Bart demonstrated by holding one arm parallel to the ground and the other angled below it. "I knew approximately how high I was flying and how fast. So I knew about how far away from the subjects I needed to be before releasing the glirp."

"You mean there is a formula for glirping someone?" Roy asked.

"Sure," Bart said. "You can't release it when you are right on top of the target. You'll completely miss. You have to figure in your speed, height, and distance from the target to achieve maximum glirp coverage. It's all science and numbers. Like the birds, I glirp with a purpose and a target in mind."

"I bet you glirped them on the first try . . . didn't you?"

"Of course," Bart said with a chuckle. "It was brilliant. They didn't know what hit them. One guy got it right in the back of the head and the other right on his backside. The rest were lucky. But they were so scared, they ran away like a bunch of ants that had their pile stepped on."

"Did they see you?"

"If they did, they probably thought I was a bird—a big one." Bart snorted. "But I swooped down quickly behind some tall pines, so they couldn't have gotten a good look at me. Besides, who's going to tell someone they were pooped on by a giant bird in a graveyard when they were vandalizing the place?"

"I don't think they would tell anyone even if they weren't vandalizing the place," Roy said. Between laughs, the two friends came up with at least 100 ideas about what the vandals must have been thinking when the glirp slapped them from behind.

"You really are a superhero," Roy said. "You need a

superhero name—a cool one." Roy waited for a reaction from Bart.

"Yeah . . . I don't know . . . maybe." Bart scrunched his face and looked away. "I'm not good with names. I don't think anyone would be impressed with a superhero named The Feathered Flyer or Wings of Wonder."

"Those aren't so bad," Roy replied, trying not to laugh. "How about the Turdinator or Glirpoman?" Giving Bart his worst ones first.

"Or Winged Poop Shooter," Bart added, while jumping to his feet.

"Night Blaster or Blob Bomber," Roy exclaimed, laughing and rolling onto his back.

"Wait, I've got it—The Flying Glirper!" Bart added in a silly tone, running around the attic in a circle, flapping his arms. "Or better yet, Gliding Glirpglooper, or Feathered Goo Glopper." Still running around the attic, Bart grabbed some feathers and tossed them in the air. "See, I told you I wasn't good at this. No one is going to feel safe with The Diving Glopbomber watching over the city, or The Fluffy Feathered SlopShooter . . ."

"The Soaring Phantom!" Roy exclaimed, minus the silly attitude.

"The Soaring Phantom," Bart imitated in a childish fashion, continuing to run in circles. "The Soaaarrrinnng Phaaaantooom," he said again, in a swirl of feathers. Then he stopped directly in front of Roy, looked to the ceiling, and mumbled to himself, "The Soaring Phantom . . . huh . . . that's pretty good, kid. Actually, it's really good. Yeah . . . The Soaring Phantom. I like it."

"I thought you might like it," Roy replied. "Except you could spell 'phantom' with an 'f' instead of a 'ph'. It would make it more unique, and you could have the initials 'SF'. You could put them on your vest or something."

"I feel like a different person when I fly. So, why not have a different name? The Soaring Fantom—I'm off, into the sky to wipe out crime from way up high!" Bart proclaimed, standing stiffly with his hands on his hips.

Roy kneeled next to Bart, aimed his arms out towards him, and proclaimed, "The Soaring Fantom—fighter of crime." Bart grabbed a roll of slender, red tape from a box and walked towards the Majestic Flyer. He began tearing off finger-length strips and placing them on the flyer. Roy tilted his body far left and right but couldn't see what his friend was doing. In no time, Bart stepped back to reveal the letters "S" and "F" diagonally positioned across the upper right flap of the molded vest. Roy smiled. Bart turned around and smiled back.

As Roy admired the ragged letters, his carelessness with time startled him again. The Ooberleeben read 5:18 a.m. It was time to go, but not before he asked Bart one last question, "What's it like to fly?"

Bart seemed eager to respond. "I guess it's like you'd imagine—but not scary at all. It's peaceful and quiet and free. I'm not good with words, and even if I were, I don't think the words exist to describe the feeling properly. It's something you have to experience for yourself."

"Yeah, I bet," Roy said.

Bart looked right at Roy. "Maybe you'll know someday—anything's possible."

Roy's eyes widened. "Really? You think?"

"Maybe," Bart said, following Roy down the attic stairs. "But for now, you should get home. Don't want to spoil the night by getting caught."

Just the tiniest possibility of Roy flying made him flush and tingly. Still, he kept his response casual. "Yeah . . . whatever. You're the boss."

CHAPTER 12

THE NEXT 379.5 HOURS

Roy felt in complete control of his summer days. During the week, he spent most of his time with Nicholas. Occasionally, he had to fight back the urge to tell his best friend about his nights with Bart. Especially since Nicholas wouldn't stop bragging about his upcoming trip to Japan. He had an aunt that lived there, and his family was going to pay her a visit in early August. She had all kinds of cool adventures scheduled for them, and Roy often struggled to hide his envy. If he could only tell Nicholas about his unbelievable summer, then he would be the one talking while Nicholas listened in amazement. But Roy couldn't tell Nicholas anything. And that was that.

On the weekends, Roy helped his dad tackle the many home improvement projects his mom wanted finished before the new school year. His list of adventures had become a distant memory, and his mom painstakingly made plans for a family trip to Uncle Bill's the third week in August.

So his presentation would be lame. At least he could keep a secret. Most of the kids he knew would've blabbed about Bart and his flyer the first night they met him just to impress the popular crowd. Roy knew better. Nothing was worth giving away Bart's secret—not even a permanent spot at the cool kids' lunch table.

Roy's summer nights were right on track as well. Like clockwork, he snuck to Bart's every night. Bart didn't mention the possibility of him flying, and Roy didn't dare bring up the subject. Most of the time, Bart went on missions while Roy stayed behind with Shirley. Glirping opportunities were limited, as the citizens of their small town were mostly law-abiding, honest folks. Even though Roy was pleased to know he lived in such a safe community, he did wish Bart had more crime-fighting moments.

Every night Bart returned from a mission, he gladly filled Roy in on all the action. Although the headsets were working well, Bart had to concentrate on the task at hand and often forgot to communicate with mission control. Roy didn't mind. He waited patiently for Bart's return when he could hear all about the Soaring Fantom's crime fighting efforts. Roy could listen for hours as Bart recalled mission after mission.

During one return flight home, he had a flock of geese following him. "They were squawking loudly and drawing attention to themselves," Bart said. "I tried swooping down low and dodging in and out of trees, but they still managed to trail me. There must have been twenty of them. Luckily, when I came in for a landing and dropped below the tree line, they made a sharp right turn, and I lost them. Man . . . what a relief. I wasn't sure what I was going to do with twenty geese on my roof."

Then there was another mission where Bart was sure someone shot at him. "I was soaring peacefully over some dense woods when I heard 'POW . . . POW.' I was sure the noises were gunshots, and the bullets were aimed in my direction."

"Did they think you were a duck?" Roy asked.

"I'm not sure. But I got out of there as quickly as I could—and I haven't flown out that way since," Bart said. "I'm not taking any chances."

Despite Bart's run in with geese and guns, his enthusiasm for fighting crime never wavered. He had many missions that made all his efforts worthwhile, with one in particular he was especially proud of.

"I heard an alarm going off, so I went towards the direction of the noise," Bart began in a suspenseful tone. "Sure enough, there was a person running out of a broken window in Cecil's Drugstore with a stash in his hands. I coasted behind him and unloaded two quick blasts of glirp directly on top of him. He didn't know what hit him. He was running around in circles, flailing his arms—he looked like a liquid ghost." Bart slurred his words through bouts of laughter. "He finally fell to the ground, and I flew out of sight right as the police arrived."

That mission, by far, was Bart's most notable, and Roy was certain the events would get the town's attention. He was right. The incident made the front page of the local paper. There was no mention of a bird, and very little was said about the glirp. The police assumed the robber had accidentally spilled something on himself while hurrying out of the store. Turns out, the man was responsible for a slew of burglaries in the area. But not anymore—thanks to the Soaring Fantom.

Yet, after a few weeks of missions around town, Bart needed a change of scenery. By late July, he was determined to make it up the road to the big city. Bigger cities had more people, so there was bound to be more crime.

One rainy night, Bart and Roy hunkered down in the attic making minor tweaks to the flyer in preparation for the longer flight. Roy was now an expert at threading feathers and checking the aluminum frame for any signs of weakness. By helping Bart, Roy felt as though he was (in a small way) fighting crime, too.

The best summer of his life was literally flying by, and Roy hadn't given much thought to everything coming to an end. When they first met, he hadn't paid much attention to Bart's moving plans. Now, he was almost too afraid to confirm it was really going to happen.

"Bart?" Roy asked softly while inspecting a row of newly threaded feathers. "How much longer before you move?"

"Well, it's definitely countdown time," Bart said. "I have about five weeks left—before I have to start my new job."

Roy's face sank. "Only five weeks, huh?"

"Yep—five weeks. But a lot can happen in that time. Maybe, before I move, we can go on a mission together."

"Really . . . you think?"

"Maybe a short mission, but we'd have to get those smaller wings ready, and I'd have to modify one of my old vests for you. It would be a lot of work," Bart said.

"Think you're up for it?"

"Are you kidding?" Roy jumped up. "I am more than ready."

"Whoa there now. Let me look at some things tomorrow—to make sure I can make everything work. I need to take some measurements." Bart stood up and walked over to a nearby folding table. "Don't get too excited. I might not be able to get a flyer together in time. Maybe I shouldn't have said anything. I'd hate to get your hopes up, kid."

"No, it's okay . . . really . . . I understand."

Bart grabbed a tape measure from the table and wrapped it around Roy's chest. "Like I said, I need to look at a few things. For now, let's weigh you and get some more measurements." He scribbled the numbers on his hand with an Invisoscript. "Okay, let's get you on the scale downstairs, and then you need to get on home."

After Bart recorded all the information he needed, Roy sloshed back to his house in the cool rain and struggled up the slippery fire escape. He hid his wet clothes at the bottom of the laundry basket and slid into bed. His mind was racing. Thinking about flying and Bart moving all in the same night felt like World War III in his head. He didn't have the energy to fight the battle of emotions he was dealing with. So, he slept instead.

Later that morning, Roy went with his mom and Melonie to shop for his dad's birthday. His mom wanted to buy him a new drill he had been hinting at for most of spring and summer. Unlike Bart, his dad had every tool imaginable. He wasn't a naturally gifted handyman, but with the right equipment, he could fool just about anyone into thinking he was. On the other hand, Bart didn't need fancy tools. Most of his gear and supplies had been other people's junk or trash. Constructed from aluminum scraps, found bird feathers, molded plastic, string, and Velcro, the Majestic Flyer was no exception. Both men were certainly deserving of admiration, though Roy felt he got an extra dose of inspiration from Bart.

CHAPTER 13

THE NEXT 14 HOURS

After his dad's birthday dinner, cake, and presents, all the Winklesteens disappeared into their rooms for bed. Roy was happy to have an early night to himself. He wondered if Bart could pull together the proper wing size and vest to make him a flyer. Was he too heavy? Too light? Maybe he should have sucked air in or out to make his chest bigger or smaller. Did Bart really think he deserved to fly like a bird?

Roy slid down the fire escape and over to Bart's side door. The more he thought about what Bart may have decided, the faster his heart thumped. He made his way inside and poked his head through the attic opening. Shirley greeted him with a brief lick on the cheek. Bart didn't notice him right away, so Roy had time to note a smaller flyer lying on the attic floor. The wings were shorter and covered with an assortment of colorful feathers. They looked similar to a pair Roy had seen resting against the attic wall. The vest had many more Velcro straps than Bart's and its profile was flat and bulky.

"Roy, there you are. C'mon up, I have something to show you." Bart reached for the smaller flyer. "Want to try it on?"

Roy didn't know what to say. He felt numb. Bart had actually worked on a flyer especially for him. He held out his arms and let Bart adjust, pull, and tighten as needed. "How does that feel? The wings need some work, but you can make some adjustments while I'm on my missions," he said.

"Feels great," Roy mumbled.

"Not too tight right here, is it? I know the vest doesn't conform to your body, but a thick sweater might fill in the gaps and make it more comfortable and secure." Bart shifted the vest to align with Roy's body. "Wow. Is that what I look like?" he said with a wondering stare. "I guess I never really looked at myself in the mirror."

As Bart continued to inspect the makeshift flyer, Roy began feeling strange—almost sick. The cause was obvious, and he decided he might as well face the truth.

It was the only way he was going to feel better. He DIDN'T deserve any of this. He hadn't spent over 71,000 hours since the age of 12 working on a flyer. He wasn't even 12 yet. Bart shouldn't be looking at him in HIS invention. He should never have to look at anyone, other than himself, in it. He was the only one worthy of wearing it.

"I—I don't know," Roy began.

"What? What don't you know?" Bart asked.

"I shouldn't be doing this," Roy said. "It's not right."

"It'll be fine. It just needs a little tweaking. But you can handle that—there's time."

"No . . . that's not what I mean. You're right, it should only be you flying," Roy said. "It should always be that way. No one else ought to have the opportunity. They didn't work for it." Roy began sliding his arms out of the wing loops. "I understand now—why you don't want to tell anyone you succeeded. People don't deserve to know. They'll never appreciate your hard work. They'd just take the special away and sell it for a buck."

"Wait . . . kid," Bart said with a satisfied grin. "I'm not going lie. I did think that, maybe, you didn't deserve to fly. But even if I had my doubts, I don't anymore. You just proved to me you DO deserve to fly." Bart guided Roy's arms back through the loops. "You finally understand, and that's all that matters. I know you will never take my hard work for granted. You've been a loyal and trustworthy friend. And . . . come to think of it . . . that's something I've never really had." Bart stopped fidgeting with the glider and looked Roy in the eyes. "Out of all the people that could've found out my secret, I'm glad it was you. So let's get busy. You have lots of work and practice to get in before the big mission." Bart glanced at two calendars now hanging side by side on the wall next to the window.

Roy continued to stand motionless and speechless as Bart shuffled around him several times, assessing the fit of the flyer. Roy had been dreaming of this moment. Now that it was here, he didn't know what to think.

Bart unstrapped the flyer from Roy's body and began pointing out all the adjustments needed. Roy knew he should be listening, but he couldn't find the space in his mind for any more information. Instead, in a trancelike state, he took small and calculated steps towards the calendars Bart must have filled in earlier that day. He stared at all of the scribbles and slashes through the boxes representing their time together. The left one was July, the right August. A sloppy, red circle encompassed the August 14th box. At the top, it read "Roy flight." That day represented both a first and a last in their friendship. It was to be their first and only mission together and their last night together. At the bottom of the August 14th box, it read "move."

"See how tight the schedule is?" Bart said. "I figure we need every day until the mission to tweak the flyer and get in practice time. If the weather seems iffy, we can adjust some things, but I think my last night here would be the best night for a flight together, don't you? Kind of a great way to end our summer—if you ask me."

"Yeah," Roy murmured. "I guess we'd better get busy."

Bart dedicated so much of the night showing Roy how to shorten the wings and solder the aluminum frame together that no time remained for him to complete a mission. Roy tried extra hard to show his appreciation. He wanted to fly, but more, he wanted Bart to stay put. If only Bart had filled in the calendar with the Invisoscript, it all wouldn't seem so permanent.

Bart was going to move, summer was going to be over, and Roy's life was going to go back to being what it had always been.

As he left Bart's and headed for home, it was the first time all summer Roy wasn't happy. While getting ready for bed, his sadness swiftly turned to anger. To Roy, life seemed so random and unfair—completely illogical. He had finally found someone a lot like him, a truly best friend, who was leaving the day after the most exciting event of his life was scheduled to take place—with his new best friend. Could life be any more ridiculous? How could something as complex as living seem to have no balance or proper distribution? Everything good always ended too soon and everything bad seemed to hang around forever. Mathematically, it didn't make sense. And no matter how hard he tried, he would never be able to come up with a formula to fix it. Even Bart couldn't cure the disease of unfairness life seemed to suffer from. Feeling helpless, Roy let out one last sigh and allowed himself to sleep.

It wasn't long before he awoke to the smell of cherry lip gloss. Roy barely opened his sticky eyes to find Melonie staring at him. "Want some?" she asked, grinning from ear to ear while she attempted to slather some more of the shiny stuff on her plump lips. Evidently, she lacked a clear sense of her facial geography, because she looked like she'd devoured an entire plate of fried chicken without using her hands.

"How many times have I told you, Mel, stay out of my room," Roy managed to remind her with what little bit of energy he could summon. "Now get out and leave me alone."

"It's Melonie—not Mel. Mel is a boy's name, and I'm no boy," she said, stiff-armed with her lips pursed. "Mom said to 'get up.' Dad needs your help in the garage. Then, maybe you can play house with me. If you're nice, I'll let you pull me and my dolls around in the wagon and we can pretend we are going on a trip."

"Go away, M-E-L-O-N-I-E." Roy chucked a pillow towards her. "Tell Mom I'll be there in a minute." She disappeared down the hall, and Roy crawled out of bed, rubbing his eyes until his best daylifer face emerged.

CHAPTER 14

THE NEXT 43.5 HOURS

Roy spent all morning helping his dad replace the window shutters on the front of the house. After lunch, they moved all the supplies to the side of the house so they could replace those shutters as well. Roy helped his dad position the ladder underneath his bedroom window. The view looking up at the modestly detailed opening was not nearly as interesting as the view looking out of it—but Roy kept that thought to himself.

After the first window was finished, Roy grabbed both sides of the ladder. His plan was to lift it slightly off the ground and slide it under the other window, where his dad was waiting. But right as he started walking, the top of the ladder began to fall away from the house.

"Look out!" his dad yelled. Roy ducked and covered his head, and his dad jumped out of the way. The ladder slammed into the big oak tree, where it rolled off a branch and onto the ground.

"Good thing the ladder is light," his dad said with a sigh of relief. "Here . . . help me get it to the window." Both guys lifted the ladder and aimed it towards the window. During the maneuver, the ladder grazed the biggest branch on the tree, knocking and untucking the end of the fire escape. The lower part of the weathered rope landed on top of Roy's head and shoulders like a drunk python. Roy froze and waited for his dad's response.

"Huh . . . I'd forgotten we'd installed this thing." His dad lifted the rope off Roy and gave it a few tugs. "Doesn't seem very safe—and it looks like an animal has been chewing on the knot up there."

Roy took a deep breath and tried to remain calm. Even though the whole incident seemed innocent enough, he still felt guilty. "I'll go upstairs and wind it around the branch really well so it doesn't get in our way." Roy started towards the back door.

"Wait . . . don't bother." His dad continued to inspect the rope. "Your mom would have a fit if she knew this raggedy old thing was all you had to get out of the house during a fire. I saw one of those collapsible, emergency ladders at the store. We can go get one after we finish up here." He grabbed hold of the rope like he was going to climb it. "That's a much safer solution. This thing is useless, except maybe to a burglar."

"I'm sure it would be okay during a fire," Roy said. "The other thing seems like a waste of money for something that will probably never happen."

"Nah, they're not expensive. And your mom will like the fact that I spent money on something for your safety instead of another toy—I mean tool—for me." He looked at Roy with a grin. "Go get me the hedge clippers. I'm going to get rid of this thing."

Roy could feel his cheeks getting flush. He felt light-headed. He would never be able to sneak out of the house with a clanky, metal ladder hanging from his windowsill. Just getting it out of his closet would wake up the whole neighborhood. He had to think fast. "Hedge clippers . . . that's going to work?"

"I don't know what else would work any better." His dad looked towards the garage. "Just go get them."

Roy ran into the garage. He knew exactly where his dad kept the clippers, but he banged around for a while as if he were looking for them. He needed some time to come up with a way to stop his dad from snipping his lifeline to Bart's.

"Roy . . . come on now. We need to get busy." Roy

could tell his dad was losing his patience.

Roy ran back to the tree with the clippers. His dad already had the ladder leaning against the thick branch right next to where the rope was tied. "Hold on to the clippers for a second. Maybe I can untie it." His dad made his way up the ladder. He tried loosening the triple knot, but years of outside gunk had glued the overlapping loops together. "I figured that wouldn't work. Hand me the clippers."

Roy had no choice. He stretched out his arm and handed his dad what he now thought had to be the worst tool ever invented.

His dad separated the blades of the clippers and clamped down on the rope right below the knot. Roy could feel a drop of sweat roll down his jaw. His dad opened them wider and clamped down even harder. Roy could feel another drop of sweat rolling down the other side of his jaw. His dad clamped down again . . . and again . . . and again. A few of the nylon strands broke apart, but not enough to make a dent in the thick rope. "I need to sharpen these things."

"Charles . . . Roy, where are you?" his mom called from the front door.

"We're around here," his dad yelled back.

Roy's mom made her way to the tree and firmly

whispered. "The toilet's backed up again. It's making a mess."

His dad hurried down the ladder and threw the clippers on the ground. "Why are you whispering, honey?" He seemed flustered over her lack of urgency. "Why didn't you just yell from the door?"

Roy trailed behind his panicked parents. Unlike his dad, he knew exactly why his mom was whispering. She wasn't about to risk the possibility of the neighbors finding out the Winklesteens had toilet issues.

They all made it inside and into the downstairs bathroom. Water was everywhere, and it took his mom and dad the rest of the afternoon to clean up the mess and fix the toilet. By the time his dad had finally finished up, it was almost time to eat. Roy could tell his parents were more than done with home improvement projects for the day, so he offered to bring in all the supplies from outside—which made his dad very happy.

Roy put everything back where it belonged, except the clippers. He hid them behind a container on one of the highest shelves in the garage. Afterwards, he ran upstairs to his room and pulled the fire escape into the tree. This time, he made sure that a category five tornado wouldn't blow the end loose. Charles Royston Winklesteen II was a busy man, and Roy knew that as long as the rope was out of his dad's sight, it would be out of his mind. He closed his window and sat down on his wooden chest. Saved by the toilet, he thought.

Not long after dinner, all the Winklesteens retired to their rooms. It had been an exhausting day and the night had actually snuck up on Roy. He needed to get some sleep before his 2:00 a.m. sprint to Bart's house. This time, his brain was just as tired as his body, and he fell asleep in seconds.

Later at Bart's, all effort quickly turned towards Roy's flier. The wings needed to be shortened and leg support forms needed to be made. Bart wanted to fly that night, so they focused on the leg casts first. Roy could work on the wings while Bart went on his mission.

"I am going to cover your thighs in petroleum jelly," Bart explained. "That way the plaster won't stick to your skin." The jelly was slippery, the plaster was cold, and the whole process tickled like crazy. Roy found it almost impossible not to laugh. Nevertheless, he didn't. On the outside, he stayed cool and collected. Sometimes Roy wasn't sure if Bart realized how young he really was. Calling him "kid" and thinking he was a kid were two separate things as far as Roy was concerned.

"Okay, now that I've got the molds, I can pour the plastic tomorrow and we should be able to assemble the vest tomorrow night," Bart said as he inspected the white, powdery forms. "Now, to my mission. There has been a change of plans. Tonight, I am going to try to get to the big city." Bart started to suit up. "You keep working, and I'll get ready."

Although surprised by the abrupt schedule change, Roy knew Bart had his reasons. He was both excited and worried. This was Bart's most daring mission yet, and Roy couldn't help but recall the night Bart never returned.

"I will be out of radio range. Don't worry about me," Bart handed Roy the headset. "If I'm not home by the time you have to leave, I'll see you tomorrow . . . okay?"

Roy nodded.

The takeoff was smooth and uneventful. They kept in contact for a while, but soon Bart's voice broke up more than usual, with nothing but silence following. Roy tried to take his mind off of what might be happening to Bart by threading new feathers onto the end of the redesigned wing. Shirley lay next to him snoring, while her chomped off ear twitched from time to time. Every five minutes, Roy checked the Ooberleeben. The numbers seemed to be changing so slowly that for a moment Roy thought his beloved watch was broken. It wasn't. Instead, it turned out to be nothing more than another one of life's quirky injustices where time always went by excruciatingly slow when you're forced to wait.

Roy's entire body jerked when Bart's crackling voice finally came through his earpiece.

"Roy, come in, Roy."

"Yeah, I'm here. What's going on?"

"Success to the Soaring Fantom."

"Can't wait to hear all about it!"

"Not tonight." Bart had an insistent tone to his voice. "You need to get on home."

"But . . . why? It's only three o'clock."

"Trust me. Get on home."

Disappointed, Roy knew better than to question Bart's instructions. Sometimes, he sensed Bart was testing him. And for every test Bart threw his way, Roy didn't want to just pass it, he wanted to ace it. "See you tomorrow, then," Roy said.

Reluctantly, he went home, where the next 18 hours felt like 18 days. Roy's head filled with all sorts of questions and scenarios. Why didn't Bart let him wait in the attic? Was the mission really successful? Did Bart have to make a crash landing? Maybe he was too tired to fly home and didn't want to admit it. Or perhaps everything had gone as planned, and Bart really was testing him. That had to be it. It was all a big test. Everything was fine, and Roy had further proven to Bart he was trustworthy and could follow instructions. If Bart had any lingering doubts about letting him fly, they should all be gone now.

The next night, Roy was extremely relieved to see his friend in one piece, anxious to reveal all the details of his mission. He took his usual spot on the attic floor. Bart got comfortable across from him. He grabbed his knees and leaned in towards Roy like what he was about to say was so intense he had to brace himself.

"The flight was a lot tougher than I thought it would be," Bart began. "But, man, was it worth it. Right when my arms were about to give out, the city came into view. It was incredible." Bart closed his eyes and lifted his chin, like he was meditating or something. "The lights . . . tall buildings . . . it was all so beautiful and calm. For a moment, I didn't think it was really happening." Bart dropped his chin and his eyes popped open. "It was a heck of a view, for sure, but I had to rest. My arms were like jelly, and I was losing altitude. So the first low building I saw was where I landed."

"You had to land on a building?" Roy asked.

Bart coolly shrugged his shoulders. "Yea, but it all worked out."

"Do you think anyone saw you or heard you?"

"I don't think so. A lot of the buildings around looked abandoned. So it wound up being a safe place for me to take a break."

"How long did you stay up there?"

"Just long enough to get the feeling back in my arms," Bart said.

Roy couldn't believe what he was hearing. It all sounded so daring, yet Bart acted as if it was no big deal. Was Bart really that fearless? And did he expect Roy to be the same way? As Bart began describing all the sights and sounds he detected from the building's roof, Roy began to wonder. Was he fearless enough to fly? Did the quiet, forgettable boy who was afraid of anything with more than four legs, who only stopped sleeping with a nightlight a year ago, who still teared up when getting a shot, who had yet to ride the scariest ride at the amusement park, who bailed on a dare to eat the school cafeteria mystery meat, and who was born to over-protective parents that would gladly keep in him in an air-tight bubble if given the option, have what it takes to soar through the air like a bird? He obviously wasn't as fearless as Bart. Yet, he had to be more fearless than most other kids his age. After all, he was in a real superhero's attic, in the middle of the night, listening to true crime-fighting stories most people never thought possible. How many people could say that?

"I gave the glirp handles a squeeze," Bart said. Roy blinked his eyes back into the moment. He was missing everything. Focus, Roy thought to himself. Bart crossed his arms and clutched his biceps. "All systems were good to go—including my arms."

"Did you know what part of the city you wanted to go to?" Roy asked intently, relieved Bart hadn't seemed to notice that his mind had wandered for a moment.

"I took off from the south side of the building and circled above until I had enough altitude to miss the tallest buildings," Bart said. "They weren't that tall, but they were definitely bigger than anything around here."

"I know exactly which ones you're talking about," Roy said. "We go there every year for Christmas shopping. Those buildings are tall."

"I guess," Bart said. "But I hadn't been flying that long when I saw two guys using a metal bar to try to break into a truck."

"Did they get in it?"

"They didn't have a chance. I swooped down between the buildings and got them good. Three quick blasts—it got all over them and the car. They ran away like little babies who looked like they had spit up all over themselves."

"Justice was served," Roy said. "I bet they don't try to break into a car for a while."

"The truck may need a good washing, but at least it was where the owner left it," Bart said. "Anyway, I knew I had to get out of there."

"How'd your arms feel?"

"Rubbery." He shook his arms like he was trying to dry them. "But I caught a tailwind on the way back, so the return home was a lot easier."

"Are you going on a mission tonight?" Roy asked, fairly confident in the answer.

"Are you kidding? My arms are so sore I could barely bring skinny Shirley up the stairs."

They both laughed. Roy was glad Bart wasn't flying tonight. He didn't have the strength to worry about anything else.

They spent the rest of the night working on Roy's flyer. The wings were almost complete, so their attention turned to the vest. Bart removed the plastic leg supports from their molds. "Perfect," Bart said as he thoroughly inspected the pieces. "Let's get them attached."

He laid out the vest-in-progress and showed Roy how overlapping the supports at the base of the vest and attaching them with a single screw provided a lightweight solution to supporting a person's legs during flight. That's what Roy admired about Bart's thinking—it was so simple, almost obvious, but most people didn't have the mind to see such solutions.

"Let's try it on. C'mon over here and hold your arms out." Roy jumped up and stood like a mannequin as Bart slid the vest onto his shoulders and fastened the Velcro straps on the side and in front. Then he took each of the finished wings and bolted them onto the vest hinges. Roy slid his arms through the loops on the wings and began flapping them slowly.

"Well, how do you like it?" Bart asked, his smile so big almost every tooth was on display.

"It feels like it was made especially for me. I'm ready to FLY." Roy flapped harder.

"Not so fast," Bart said. "The flyer might be ready, but you're not. You have a lot of practicing to do and very little time to do it. So, tomorrow we get started—understand?"

"Got it, I'm ready," Roy said.

"You're going to need to get some flexibility in your shoulders and as much upper-body strength as you can build up over the next few weeks. Here, let me show you." Bart bent at the waist so his torso was parallel with the floor. He let his arms hang freely and then lifted them straight out on either side until they reached above his back. "Find a couple of heavy books and put one in each hand. That should give you enough weight to build up some strength."

Roy positioned himself like Bart and began imitating the arm motions.

"You've got it," Bart said. "Do it until it burns, and in a few weeks you'll be surprised how much it will help—flying and all."

"I'll get started when I get home," Roy said. "Well . . . maybe after I sleep a little."

"Yep, you'd better get your sleep. Flying boot camp is going to take every bit of energy you have. Now get on home."

Roy snuck back through his window, stuffed with excitement for what was to come. Sure, he had a long way to go before he was ready to leap off Bart's roof. But when the time came, he would be ready. Wouldn't he?

CHAPTER 15

THE NEXT 242 HOURS

The following days were painfully fun for Roy. He and Nicholas played hard together, often leaving him exhausted in the evenings. No matter how much his flying secret nagged to be heard, Roy kept quiet. The more time he spent with Bart, the more he understood and appreciated why some things were better left untold.

When he wasn't with Nicholas, Roy was working on his strength and flexibility training like Bart had shown him. The workouts made him sore the first few days, but soon he was able to lift larger books, more times, with less effort. Bart even noticed Roy was becoming stronger. No matter how hard Bart worked him during boot camp, Roy never let out a whimper. Sometimes it was hard for Roy to hide his feelings. One time, he almost cried. Learning how to fly was brutal.

On the first night of training, they snuck into Bart's private, fenced backyard, where Bart disappeared into a storage shed. A few minutes later, he dragged out an old gymnastics vault and placed it right in the center of the yard. Like most things Bart acquired, he'd gotten the vault for free, from a local gym that was closing.

"Can you believe this was someone's trash?" Bart said as he dusted off the worn leather surface. "I mean, look at this thing. It's still in great shape. It helped me learn to fly, and now it's going to help you."

Roy felt his pit stains getting bigger and bigger, and he hadn't done anything yet. This is it, he thought. Up until now, Bart had been the one impressing Roy with his mind-blowing inventions and superhero feats. Now, the spotlight was on Roy. Tonight was his chance to prove to Bart (and himself) that he deserved to fly. That he should fly.

"Now, stand right here," Bart said as he scraped a line with his shoe on the damp grass about 20 feet from the end of the vault. "All you have to do is bend at the waist, run towards the vault, leap at this point with your wings positioned right above your shoulders, and then kick your legs back and rest them in the supports as you land on the center of the vault on your stomach."

Piece of cake, Roy thought, sure he would ace the move on the first try—second at the most.

In what seemed like a gazillion punishing tries later, he was far from perfecting the move. The first few tries, he didn't leap high enough and landed face first into the end of the vault. The next 13 tries, he managed to land correctly, but wasn't able to get his legs positioned in time. By the 28th try, Roy landed right in the middle of the vault with his legs resting in the supports. He was quite proud of himself until Bart pointed out his failure to position his wings above his shoulders.

"You must have your wings up as your feet leave the ridge or you won't be able to push down to get the proper lift you need as you leap off the roof." When Roy heard the word "roof," something clicked. Visions of Bart's near-miss takeoff flashed through his head. In a few weeks, he was going to be leaping off a roof, three stories high. How had he forgotten to figure that not so little detail into the equation? Upon that realization, Roy became a leaping machine, with his next six attempts ending with impeccable placement and form.

"That's it. That's it!" Bart whispered with relieved enthusiasm. "You need lots of practice, but you are well on your way." The two friends shared a series of high fives. "That's enough for tonight."

Sweaty, drained, and achy all over, Roy agreed. They returned to the attic, where Bart suited up for a flight, and Roy settled in to replace feathers that had come loose during his rough landings on the vault.

Bart's mission turned out to be a quiet one. There was no need to engage the GlirpBlaster or exercise any perilous superhero moves. Instead, the mission proved to be more inspirational. "I was flying over the park, when I saw a group of deer. They looked so peaceful—not a care in the world," Bart said softly, while staring into space. "It's like they knew the park was theirs at night and no human would dare bother them. Somehow, I was a part of them—part of the wildlife. For the first time, I felt like I knew what it was like to be a bird."

Roy listened in awe as Bart continued to recall every moment of the mission in poetic detail. "Did the deer know you were flying over them?"

"Maybe spiritually . . . but they never looked up or seemed threatened in any way," Bart said. "If they felt my presence, it didn't frighten them—like a real bird wouldn't frighten them. It was like I entered another dimension where I didn't have to think about flapping my wings. It all came to me naturally. I feel like I have finally become a creature of the sky." Bart sucked in a deep breath. "I hope you get the chance to have that feeling."

Roy couldn't have agreed more.

Over the next few nights, Roy's leap onto the vault showed great promise. So, Bart decided it was time to move to the next phase of training. By the time Roy arrived at the side door, Bart had everything set up in the backyard. When Roy saw two picnic tables with a narrow plank of wood straddled between them, he knew exactly what he was going to have to do. That plank of wood could only represent one thing—the narrow roof ridge he had seen, or heard, Bart wobble down night after night.

"Okay, now's the time to see how effective your leap really is," Bart said. "Let's get your flyer on and get you up there." Bart helped Roy suit up, and before he knew it, he was standing on the picnic table staring down at the narrow plank, which from Roy's perspective seemed more like a single string of dental floss. It looked way too narrow and flimsy to support a 75 pound boy.

Roy looked hesitant.

"It's no big deal. You can start off on the wide part of the table, balance on the plank, and then leap off the end of the other table," Bart explained. "This gives you the chance to get a feel for what it will be like to run on something narrow while pushing off a wider surface."

"I got this," Roy whispered with nervous confidence.

"Okay," Bart started. "When you leap off, I will be at the end to guide you—even catch you if needed. It is going to feel strange, but I want you to get used to getting your legs up and feeling the lift your wings get."

With Bart's words in mind, Roy trotted down the table, onto the plank, and towards the end of the second table. His balance was in check, but when he got to the end, he didn't have the nerve to swing his legs behind him and into the supports. Instead, he barely jumped off with his legs dangling, hitting the ground hard, then tumbling to his knees.

He did the exact same thing seven more times.

"Keep trying," Bart said. "I know it's not easy to rely on your wings, but give them a chance. Trust me. Just remember, I am there to catch you if something goes wrong."

Trust, Roy thought. That's what this was all about. He trusted Bart, and he had a reasonable amount of trust in his leap. Now it was time to trust his wings.

Roy took a deep breath. He trotted down the plank and pushed off the edge of the table. Like the time at the pool he transformed his tentative, belly flop into a full-on dive, Roy stopped thinking about what he was doing and just did it. Before he realized it, his legs were resting in the supports and he was parallel to the ground. Bart jumped out of the way and watched Roy glide completely across the yard. Like a pro, he slid his legs back out of the supports, right in time to make a soft, two-footed landing.

"That's it!" Bart said. "You were great. I don't think I could've done better."

Bart was so proud of Roy's progress, he decided not to fly that night, letting the practice session continue until right before it was time to head home. With every attempt, Roy seemed to get better and glide farther, almost colliding with the trees a couple of times.

For the rest of the week, Roy continued to improve his takeoff and gliding techniques. After each practice, Bart would go on a mission, often returning with hilarious accounts of glirping opportunities. One mission, when he blasted a litterbug driver and some mischievous teens toilet papering a yard, proved especially memorable.

"The funny thing was, after I glirped them, they were whiter than the yard they had toilet papered," Bart managed to say between breathy laughs. "I wonder what they told their parents."

"Yeah, and that car," Roy blurted out. "They probably went home and cried to their mommies when they realized how big of a bird dropped that turd on them."

"Yeah, I'm sure they thought it was some kind of alien bird," Bart said while pretending to scare Shirley with a silly face and hooked hands.

Each night Roy and Bart were together ended with more notable moments to store in memory and with Roy another day closer to flying. And one night, when he entered Bart's backyard, he knew things were about to get really serious.

CHAPTER 16

THE NEXT 32 MINUTES

"Well, here it is," Bart stated as he held his arms out like he was presenting something on a game show. "This is what I like to call the path to flight. It's the system I used to learn how to fly, and now it's your turn."

As Bart walked around the structure, shaking it for stability, Roy couldn't believe his friend expected him to leap off of the contraption before him. It wasn't much, only a pair of wooden a-frame ladders with the same narrow plank straddling between them. Roy figured that when he stood on top of the ladder, his head would fall just below the tips of the narrow evergreen trees hugging the entire fence. He wondered how Bart had managed to practice without being seen.

"Now is the time to feel what it is like to actually fly," Bart said. "Are you ready?"

"I'm ready," Roy replied with a surge of confidence. "I've been ready."

"Then get on up there and give your wings a real try. Remember . . . push down and twist the wings towards the ground like I showed you. Push and twist . . . push and twist . . . that's all you should be thinking."

"Got it," Roy assured Bart as he positioned himself at the end of the plank. As he bent down and raised his wings, he was surprised to discover how high six feet actually felt. It didn't look that high from the ground, but neither had Bart's roof until Roy popped his head through the hatch opening for the first time.

Don't think—just do, Roy reminded himself. He trotted down the plank and pushed off the end flawlessly. In fact, it was such a flawless takeoff that he soared off the end, up and over the trees, and right into the neighbor's yard, crashing into a patio table umbrella. *Screeeeeeeech, thump!* The sound of metal chairs grinding against the concrete shattered the capsule of silence that had encased the night. In seconds, the neighbor's patio window lit up. Scraped up and confused, Roy scrambled to the corner of Bart's fence and ducked out of sight, with not one millisecond to spare.

"Don't move," a voice whispered from behind. A

rough, sweaty hand covered his mouth. It was Bart. They both froze as the neighbors inspected the umbrella for clues surrounding its slightly tilted pole. After a hasty survey of the yard, the couple returned inside, convinced an animal had ventured too close to their home. Once again, the silence returned and Bart removed his hand from Roy's mouth.

"That was too close for comfort," Bart mumbled. "We've got to be more careful. Let's get out of here." They circled around Bart's fence and through the gate. "You'd better get on home. We can't afford to make another sound the rest of the night."

"I'm sorry," Roy said in a quivery whisper. "I—"

"It's okay, these things happen," Bart said. "But when they do, we have to lay low. The neighbors could still be watching. Can't afford for them to become suspicious of me now." Bart strained to see if there was any movement coming from the neighbor's house. "By the way, are you alright?"

"I'm fine," Roy said as he examined the chunks of skin dangling from his elbow. "Just mad at myself."

"Don't be. Other than the fact that you crashed into the neighbor's furniture, it was, actually, a really good flight." Bart helped Roy get out of the flyer. "Hurry, get on home. We'll try again tomorrow." Roy did exactly what Bart said. He went home.

CHAPTER 17

THE NEXT 397 HOURS

Roy continued to practice flying night after night. The patio incident became nothing more than something else the two friends shared a giggle about from time to time. With every night of boot camp, Roy improved. For most of his flights, he was able to fly in low circles, inches below Bart's tree line, safely out of sight. He also managed a few steady landings back onto the launching board, which Bart said was much more difficult to do than the actual roof landing. Roy was officially flying, not very high, but he was flying.

Bart became so dedicated to Roy's practice sessions that he rarely went on missions, which made Roy feel guilty and glad all at the same time. "I'll have plenty of opportunities to fly when I move. Right now, I'm happy working with you. Every time I see you fly, it reminds me of all the hours I spent practicing," Bart said. "You've picked it up much faster than I did. It's so much easier to learn things when you're a kid."

Even so, Roy's progress required hard work, and the harder he worked, the faster time went by, and the faster time went by, the closer the end of summer loomed. Life—sometimes all you could do was laugh at it. Getting mad at its quirky injustices obviously hadn't changed anything. As Roy saw it, life had three moods: sneaky, ridiculous, and unfair. Sometimes it was all three, or often a combination of two, but always at least one. Didn't really matter, though. Roy couldn't change it. Besides, things could've turned out much differently. Bart could've lived in another neighborhood, or worse, Roy could've been born a daylifer.

Having considered how his summer could've been, he stopped thinking about all the time he wouldn't share with Bart. Instead, he only thought about all they had done in the short time they'd had together and what they had yet to accomplish. That change in attitude put a permanent smile back on his face.

As the nights continued to pass, flying boot camp got easier as Roy got stronger. Before long, just two days remained until the mission. Was he ready to make that leap off the roof? Absolutely. Bart knew it, and so did

Roy.

All summer, Roy managed to keep all the daylifers in the dark about his secret summer adventure. As far as his parents, Melonie, and Nicholas were concerned, he was a typical kid doing typical things. Roy strutted around the house, counting down the hours until the mission.

And when his parents planned a family picnic at the park, Roy responded enthusiastically. A day at the park was sure to wear out the rest of the Winklesteens, making an early bedtime inevitable. Roy welcomed the possibility of getting to Bart's earlier than usual.

While his mom packed a picnic basket with enough food to feed everyone on their street, Roy helped his dad load a few items into the car. It was a textbook day to be outdoors. Spots of bright, white clouds mellowed the sun's scorching rays, and a large maple tree offered a permanent shady spot to spread out a worn but plush blanket. Roy and his dad immediately began showing off their Frisbee moves, while a determined Melonie struggled to push her baby buggy through the hearty grass. Back at the tree, Roy's mom methodically laid out a splendid picnic lunch worthy of a magazine cover spot. It was a typical Winklesteen outing, with enough safety, predictability, and pleasantness for everyone to enjoy.

Roy couldn't argue the fact that time with the family was typically fun—just not exciting.

That is, until the most hilarious thing that could have happened did happen.

"Bird turd! Bird turd!" Melonie yelled while running in place and holding her head.

"Yuuuuccckkkkk . . . Mommy . . . help!" Everyone ran to Melonie, who had a white and black glob of bird poop clinging to her loopy pink bow and blond hair. As Roy's mom and dad tended to his prissy sister, he did everything in his power not to laugh. He wondered what the bird was thinking when it laid one on her. Maybe it found Melonie annoying, too. Evidently, birds do poop strategically, Roy thought. He was having a hard time wiping the grin off his face. Finally, he had a funny story to tell Bart.

Once cleaned up, Melonie managed to calm down. She now had one less bow in her stash of all things frilly. Good riddance, Roy thought.

With that small drama behind them, the Winklesteens gathered on the blanket and helped themselves to the feast of delicious goodies before them. As Roy chomped into his four-meat and two-cheese sandwich, he checked out the park activity. Usually his time on the picnic blanket was spent relaxing and people watching. Today, he spent most of his time bird watching. Like buttons and zippers, he'd never really given them a second thought. They were everywhere, different colors and sizes, making all kinds of sounds, acting suspicious of everything, with their one-eyed glares and staccato movements. Roy knew he would never fly as effortlessly as any bird, but he didn't care. In less than 30 hours, he was going to get to see the world from their perspective.

"Hey, you two," Roy's dad blurted out like he was talking in his sleep. "Your mom and I have a surprise to tell you about."

"Is it a playhouse for the backyard?" squealed Melonie.

"No, sweetie," his dad said. "This is better. Your mom and I have been talking about what Roy said, you know, about us being boring and needing some adventure in our lives. Well, we think he might be right." He glanced at his wife grinning from ear to ear. "So, we've planned a trip."

"Yeah, we're going to Uncle Bill's . . . right?" Melonie asked. "So we can swim with the dolphins."

"Nope, we've decided to skip Uncle Bill's and instead go to"—his hesitation seemed to last an eternity—"the Grand Canyon!"

"Isn't that great?" his mom added, appearing to study Roy's face for an ecstatic look of approval. "We can go camping and hiking, and we can ride mules down to the bottom of the canyon. It's going to be one giant adventure. Exactly like Roy wanted."

"And to add even more excitement to the equation, we're leaving tomorrow night." His dad patted Roy on the leg. "Don't tell me we're not adventurous."

CHAPTER 18

THE NEXT 12 HOURS

Roy's mom pulled some travel brochures out of her bag. "After Dad gets off work, we're going to hop in the car and go. We'll both take turns driving all night so we'll be at the canyon in time for the sunrise."

"So, what do you guys think?" they both asked at the same time, as if they had been rehearsing this exact moment for days.

Melonie started asking a million questions. Roy didn't hear any of them. All he heard was "tomorrow night." Out of all the nights to start an adventure, his parents had to pick the one that already had the biggest adventure of his life scheduled. Is this all some colossal joke? Roy thought. At that moment, he couldn't help but revise his view on life. Instead of three moods, it now had four: sneaky, ridiculous, unfair, and just plain cruel.

That stupid list! What had he been thinking?

"Roy, you're awfully quiet," his mom said, while loading some more potato salad onto his plate.

"He's speechless, of course," his dad said with a prideful grin.

"Wow—can't wait," Roy managed to say with completely bogus enthusiasm. He wasn't about to let them know how he really felt. Besides, he couldn't blame his parents for trying. Somehow he was going to have to stop, or at least delay, this alleged adventurous trip to the Grand Canyon. There was only one solution to this problem: Bart. He would know what to do.

Just as the Winklesteens were finishing their dessert, menacing clouds began to appear at the park's edge. When a cooler wind blew a corner of the blanket onto Roy's chocolate cake, he knew the picnic was ending. Everything and everybody made it into the car right before the first drenching raindrops cannonballed onto the windshield. Roy was glad to be heading home. He needed time alone to sort out the latest wad of nonsense life had hurled his way.

He managed to hide out in his room most of the evening. He was supposed to be gathering all his dirty clothes together that needed washing for the trip. Clothes? Who could think about clothes right now? His mind was churning his thoughts like a blender. When he wasn't pacing the floor, he was peering out the window. He had no choice but to rely on Bart to come up with a plan to delay the Winklesteen Grand Canyon trip for at least a day. That was all he needed—one day.

The darkness took its sweet time getting to midnight and Roy couldn't wait another second. Despite the downpour, he made it to Bart's faster than his fastest previous time. As he charged through the side door, he was shocked at the sight before him. Boxes were everywhere. Some stacked so high, Roy couldn't see over them.

"Bart . . . where are you?" he yelled, traveling from room to room like a frantic mouse in a maze. Faint shuffling sounds eventually led him to the garage where he found his friend loading boxes into a truck.

"Hey kid, you're early . . . and soaking wet," said Bart. "What is it? You look like you've seen a ghost or something."

Roy stood in the doorway and managed to blurt out four simple words, "We have a problem." Bart stopped loading and slowly walked towards Roy.

"A problem? What sort of problem?" Bart asked, his face morphing into such extreme seriousness that his two eyebrows became one. "Talk to me, Roy."

Without moving, Roy desperately told Bart exactly what had happened at the park. "We're leaving tomorrow, after my dad gets off work. What are we going to do?" Roy asked shivering uncontrollably.

"C'mon kid, first things first. Let's get you in the house and dried off," Bart said in his calmest voice. With the help of a few towels, the two friends patted Roy down to a state of dampness. Within seconds, they locked eyes and gave each other their best "it's time to get busy" look. Each knew exactly where to head to get the mental juices flowing: the attic.

"Can't fly tonight," said Bart, gazing out the rain-spotted, attic window. "We'll have to think of something else." Hearing the determination in Bart's voice calmed Roy's pounding heart. "Don't want to blow your family's vacation." He shifted his stare towards the calendars. "Wonder if there's a way to delay it a day?"

"That's exactly what I was thinking. One day is all we need." Roy said as his mind began to clear. "If we're going to leave tomorrow, there's no reason why we can't leave the next day. What's one day? So, we're there six days instead of seven. How much time does a family need at the Grand Canyon anyway?"

"If you say so," Bart said. "It's your family."

"With a good plan, it shouldn't be a problem," Roy

said.

"A plan," Bart said, rubbing his chin and staring at the attic floor. "Let's see. What could delay a trip by just one day?" As Bart remained deep in thought, Roy acted as if he were thinking too, but all he was really doing was wondering what Bart was thinking.

After what seemed like hours later, Bart raised his right hand to chest level, pointed his finger, and cocked his head. Roy sighed in relief. He knew Bart was about to blurt out something brilliant. "You said you were at the park today, right?"

"Yeah, we were there all day. You know, playing Frisbee and eating."

"Well, you can't fake an injury, it's too late." Roy could almost hear Bart's brain humming with ideas. "But, you could fake an allergy, or a rash. Something you could have gotten from being at the park, like poison ivy." He began pacing in front of the window. "Hmm . . . not sure we can mimic poison ivy . . . but fake itching and botchy skin might do the trick."

"Yeah, then I could be all better the next day, and we could leave for the trip," Roy said.

"That might work." Bart began rummaging through the few boxes remaining in the attic. "I think I have what we need to make you look uncomfortable enough to need some rest for one day, but not miserable enough to send you to the doctor. It's risky, but it could work." Bart pulled out a sponge and half-full bottle of red dye. "If we dab this on your cheeks, you might be able to convince your parents you picked up a virus or had a reaction to something at the park."

"Yeah . . . one of those twenty-four hour viruses," Roy said sarcastically as he made himself comfortable on one of the boxes. Bart dipped the sponge in the bottle and patted it all over Roy's face. "Yeah, not too bad. The sponge makes it look more blotchy."

"It feels kind of weird and stiff," Roy said, opening his mouth real wide.

After a few minutes, Bart licked his finger and swiped it across Roy's cheek. "I was afraid that would happen."

Roy felt his face. "What's happened?"

"The dye is washing off too easily. But not to worry— I have an idea." Bart dug through the largest box in the room. He pulled out an old heat lamp, plugged it in, and set it on the floor next to Roy. "The heat should help the dye set in."

Roy leaned towards the heat of the lamp. Bart positioned himself on a box in front of Roy. Normally, they would sit down on the attic floor and work on the flyers, but everything was ready. Bart had even fixed a pair of old BinGloculars for Roy to wear.

As the two friends sat and waited, Roy realized this moment was the last time he would sit across from his friend. A sad lump filled his gut. He wondered if Bart felt the same. Would he miss him, their time together? Or was Bart so used to doing things on his own that it would be easy for him to return to his life of inventive solitude?

Roy stroked Shirley's head. Even though he had a million questions he still wanted to ask Bart, he could only remember one. The rest were hiding impishly, waiting to emerge only after he said goodbye to his best friend for the last time. "What happened to Shirley's ear?"

"Ah, I was wondering when you were going to ask me that. You waited longer than most." Bart grinned. "But, like I tell everybody who asks, I don't know. She shoved her entire head into a burrow going after a chipmunk. A few seconds later, she pulled her head out with a bloody ear. All I could do was patch her up. Shirley's the only one that knows what really happened." He rubbed the drooling dog's snout. "But I'm pretty sure it wasn't that little rodent that did the damage. I think it was something much bigger."

Roy looked directly into the dog's droopy, brown eyes. "Shirley, I sure do wish you could talk."

"Since we're asking questions," Bart interrupted with a peculiar tone to his voice. "I have one for you."

"Go ahead, ask me anything," Roy said, curious to know what information Bart could possibly want from him.

"Your friend's secret? You know . . . the one you told me about when we first met."

"What about it?"

"Well . . . what's the secret?"

"I told you." Roy tucked his hands underneath his thighs and curled his back like an angry cat. "I can't tell."

"Yeah . . . but that was before you knew me. You know me now." Bart moved the lamp to Roy's other side. "Who could I possibly tell? Better yet, why would I tell? You don't trust me? I've trusted you all this time."

"It has nothing to do with trusting you. It's not my secret to tell," Roy said, pushing the lamp away from his face. "So, that's that."

"Okay, fine. I'll drop it." Bart threw up his hands in a wave of surrender and headed towards the stairs. "Be right back."

Confused, Roy leaned into Shirley. He couldn't figure

out why Bart would ask him such a thing. If anyone knew how important it was to keep a secret, it was Bart. Did he honestly think his were the only secrets that had a place in the halls of silence? He shuddered at the thought of being angry with his friend. Considering what lay ahead, Roy decided to ignore Bart's lapse in judgment. No one's perfect, Roy thought.

Unless Bart knew exactly what he was doing.

Perhaps, this was another test—the final exam, one might say. Roy leaned back on his hands and closed his eyes. He smiled proudly. When it came to trust, he had nothing more to prove.

Bart returned to the attic with a small bowl of glirp. "Let's add a little of this to your face. It will give it more of a rashy, bumpy look." He dipped his pinky into the bowl and tapped his finger across Roy's cheeks like he was sending Morse code signals. "How does it feel?"

"Warm and kinda sticky," Roy said, scrunching his nose.

After a few more minutes of waiting, Bart licked his finger and swiped his face again. "It looks pretty convincing, but you are going to have to give the performance of a lifetime. Like there's no way you can sit in a car all night."

Roy patted his face gently, trying to feel what he

looked like. "Feels like a rash. And it does itch, so I shouldn't have to act too much."

"You can wash a little off at a time, so most of it is gone by bedtime. Hopefully, if everything goes as planned, your family trip will be back on for the next night." Bart grabbed Roy's shoulders and looked him straight in the eyes. "It's all up to you."

"No problem," said Roy, looking straight back at Bart. "I can do it. I'll hang a white cloth in my window when I get the delay in place."

"And if I don't see a white cloth?"

"Don't worry, you'll see one."

CHAPTER 19

SHOW TIME

With a plan in place, Roy and Bart spent the remainder of the night plotting out the mission. The short flight included circling above Holden's, the school, and the park. When Roy left to return home, he was careful not to say goodbye to Bart.

By the time Roy returned to his room, the rain had stopped. He turned on the light and studied his reflection in his dresser mirror. The dye and glirp definitely made him look like he was suffering from a bumpy rash. It was really starting to itch, and Roy no longer had to act uncomfortable. He truly was uncomfortable. He crawled into bed and waited. Considering the circumstances, he was quite calm.

It wasn't long before he heard his father shuffling about. Later, his mother's swift but delicate steps joined his father's, with Melonie's thumping about eventually drowning out all other sounds. Roy knew it was only a matter of time before she made her way into his room, especially today, when the excitement of packing was sure to consume every second.

Once footsteps finally arrived outside his door, Roy snapped his eyes closed and braced himself for Melonie's elephant stampede of an entrance. It's show time, Roy thought, and Melonie was the best person to practice on before the big performance.

But his door didn't swing open with thunderous footsteps tromping towards his bed. Instead, the knob turned slowly and the door creaked open. The footsteps coming towards him were light and cautious. "Roy?" He gradually opened his eyes to find his mother leaning over him with a concerned look on her face. "Do you feel okay—your face?" She gently touched his cheek.

It's now or never, Roy thought. "Ouch!" he blurted out grabbing his face.

"Sit up. You have some kind of rash." She pulled him out of bed and into the hall bathroom. Roy stared in the mirror as his mother examined him more closely. She felt his forehead and turned on the faucet in preparation to make a cold compress.

"No, don't." Roy backed away. "It will hurt—it

burns."

With a puzzled look she asked, "Well, does anything else hurt—your stomach—your head? I should call the doctor."

"No . . . it's just my face. It's probably an allergy, or a virus." He couldn't look his mom in the eyes. "I bet if stay in bed for twenty-four hours, I'll probably be better." His mom stared him down. Roy began to panic. Was she on to him? Even with her glaring eyes searing through him, Roy wasn't about to give up. "Nicholas got the same rash the last time we were at the park," he began. "I think we both got it from the bushes. But the next day, it was almost gone, and he was fine—after he stayed in bed and rested. I'm sure that's all I have to do."

"Are you sure it looks like the same rash Nicholas had?" Some of her worry wrinkles began to disappear. "Maybe I should call his mom."

"No, it's the same. I'm sure. Besides, they're in Japan," Roy swiftly replied.

"Well . . . I'm not sure what to do. You get back in bed." With a firm, flat hand on his back, she led him to his room. "I'm going call your dad."

Roy climbed into bed. He strained to listen to his mom's phone conversation. He couldn't make out what she was saying, but her tone was quite clear: concerned, with a hint of frustration. A prickly tumor of guilt lodged in Roy's throat. This lie made his kite-flying lie feel like nothing more than an irritating fuzz up the nose. Why was life forcing him to do this to his parents? His family deserved a nice trip together, and he deserved to fly. Why did everything have to be so complicated? Time wasn't even the issue, timing was. Once again, life had gotten the scheduling all wrong, and he was only trying to fix it. There's nothing to feel guilty about, Roy told himself. It wasn't his fault. Compromising his parents' good intentions was a necessary evil.

Right as he swallowed the lump, Melonie plowed through the doorway, her hands on her hips. "Mom says you have some kinda disease." She looked at him like he was road kill.

"Ewe . . . you look disgusting."

"Melonie, let your brother rest." Helen Winklesteen snapped her fingers and pointed down the hall. Before Roy could blink, the little brat was back in her room. He smiled at his mom in sheer amazement. She didn't need a magic wand to make the most annoying person in the world disappear. She had the snap, which worked every time.

"I spoke to Dad." She nudged her backside onto his bed. "He thinks he knows which bushes you're talking about. There's a coating on the leaves you might be having a reaction to." She popped off the cap to a dark brown bottle. "Take this medicine and rest. We'll postpone the trip until you feel better."

"I'm sure I'll feel better tomorrow," Roy said, trying to not act excited. "I'm sorry I've ruined the trip."

"Don't be silly, the Grand Canyon can wait." She tucked the covers tightly around him. "It's been there for thousands of years. It's not going anywhere in the next couple of days." After drawing the curtains and some minor straightening of his room, she headed out the door. "I'll bring you some soup."

Right as the door latch clicked, Roy hopped out of bed and grabbed a white t-shirt from his drawer. He hung it from the window lock and readjusted the curtains. He stood back and looked at his window. Problem solved, he thought. He closed his eyes and let out a big sigh. He felt dizzy. Sleep—he needed sleep.

CHAPTER 20

TIME TO FLY

Roy played sick all day. He was more than happy to lie around and let his mom wait on him. He needed the rest. By dinnertime, he showed signs of getting better, or so his parents thought. In reality, he had managed to scrub off most of the dried glirp and dye from his face. By bedtime, his parents seemed to agree that the Winklesteen family would be heading to the Grand Canyon the next evening. All was fine. Roy was going to fly and his parents were going to get their trip. No harm done, Roy tried to assure himself.

He headed to Bart's as soon as the coast was clear. With the exception of a few stray boxes, the moving truck was ready to go and so was Bart. The two friends didn't waste much time discussing how Roy's fake rash played out. Instead, Bart meticulously rechecked every fastener and joint on the flyers while Roy filled the blaster with a fresh batch of glirp. They worked seamlessly together like a nut and bolt, as neither seemed much use without the other. Radio sets were tested, helmets were tightened, and BinGlocular lenses were spit cleaned. Before long, it was time to fly.

"I guess this is it. Like they predicted, the weather couldn't get any better," Bart said, studying the view out the window. "Sure you want to do this?"

"Are you kidding? Nothing can stop me now," Roy replied with a nervous tinge.

"I'll go first, and then you hand me your flyer. Let's do this," Bart said with a wink. He made it onto the roof and extended his arm down through the hatch opening to retrieve Roy's flyer. Roy poked his head up above the ridge. Bart clutched the back of his shirt and pulled him up onto the roof. There was no turning back now. Roy stayed on all fours, straddling the ridge until Bart shut the hatch. The August air made no apologies for reminding them it was summer. Bart yanked Roy's arm and helped him to his feet. Even though his tennis shoes gripped the roof shingles, he was certain he would slip any second.

"I gotcha," Bart reassured him through a whisper. "Grab my arm and let's get to the chimney." Bart began suiting up. Roy clung to the chimney until it was time for him to slip into his flyer.

Bart adjusted his BinGloculars and Roy did the same. His heart was pounding in a way he'd never felt before. This moment was exactly as he had imagined it a thousand times in his head, yet nothing like how he thought it would feel.

"Stop thinking about it," Bart insisted. "Flying has become second nature to you. Your wings are your parachute. Control them, like I taught you, and you have nothing to worry about. Okay?"

"Yeah . . . okay. I'm ready."

Bart worked his way behind Roy. "You're first . . . like we discussed. I'll pass you once we're in the air. After you clear the trees, turn to the left, then look for me. I'll fly over you." Roy nodded his head in agreement. When he leaned into Bart, all his emotions suddenly whittled down into a singular, sharp point. He was petrified. His legs were numb and his sweaty hands were struggling to grasp the metal wing handles. Could he do this? Should he do this?

"I'm going to let go of you now." Again, Roy nodded his head in response. "On three—one . . . two . . . three!" And like he had done so many times before, Roy did exactly what Bart said. There was no more time to think. It was time to do. He bent 90 degrees at his waist, raised his wings, trotted down the thin ridge, and leapt off the roof. He thrust his legs behind him and slid them into the supports. As he pushed and twisted with all his might, he felt his wings grab the air. He dropped his shoulder and looked to his left.

Bart whooshed above and away from him. Roy followed two body lengths behind him, took a deep breath, and exhaled all his fears and uncertainties into the heavy night air. His takeoff was flawless and now . . . HE WAS FLYING.

"Looking good, kid." Roy heard Bart in his earpiece. "Let's circle around for a bit, then head towards the park. We need to get higher—follow me," Bart said as he pushed his wings down and headed upward. Roy did the same, but shot up well above Bart's flight path. Before he had time to panic, Bart quickly flapped his wings until he was right there with Roy.

"Feeling okay?" Bart asked.

"Fine . . . I'm fine."

"Your arms aren't cramping?"

"No, it's easy." Roy soared closer to Bart. "Can we go higher?"

"Follow me," Bart said as he thrust his wings up and down three times and headed towards the moon. Roy only had to flap his wings two times, and he was right there with Bart. He could see the entire town, and the farther he soared, the more daring he became. Being up so high didn't make his stomach queasy at all. He'd worried for nothing.

Bart was right. Flying like a bird was different from anything he had ever experienced, but as natural as walking or riding a bike. He was so sure of himself that he shifted his sight so he could see out of the magnified part of the BinGloculars. He could read street signs, see inside cars, and even detect his fellow nightlifers, of the furry kind, rummaging around in some garbage cans. For the first time in his life, the town actually looked interesting to him. The patterns, shapes, and lines all lay in harmony with hazy dots of man-made light, warping the regularity into a mysterious landscape where nothing seemed normal. For a few seconds, Roy was hypnotized, forgetting where he was and why he was there.

He hadn't noticed that Bart had soared at least two blocks away from him.

"Bart . . . Bart! I need to catch up."

"Okay, I'll circle around . . . don't panic . . . head my way." Roy, dropped his shoulder, pushed and twisted his arms, and turned his head towards Bart. Before long, the two were almost side-by-side.

"Let's see if the deer are back," Bart suggested.

"Let's go!" Roy said as he followed right behind Bart. They both leaned to the left and circled over a patch of rooftops. Roy looked straight down. He thought about all the people snuggled up in bed, completely oblivious to what was happening above them. Some of them were the very kids he hoped to impress next year. Others were the kids he'd failed to impress this year.

Boy . . . if they could see him now.

"You still okay?" Bart's voice vibrated in Roy's ear.

"I'm great. I see the park straight ahead." Roy spotted the soccer field where he and Nicholas spent most of their time. He couldn't believe how tiny it looked. It felt huge when he was actually playing soccer.

And there was the place under the tree where his parents had proclaimed how adventurous they were. Roy got chills just thinking about how this moment almost didn't happen.

"You see anything?" Bart asked.

Roy scanned the entire park. "I see them—the deer— to your right." He zoomed in on the group with his BinGloculars and headed closer to them. There were seven figures in clear view: two fawns and the rest females. They were busy grazing and didn't seem to care that winged humans were circling above them. He looked around for other wildlife, but the deer appeared to have the park to themselves. Like him, they seemed happy to be awake when so many other creatures were sleeping. The park never looked so beautiful, and the moment felt as poetic as the way Bart had described it. He couldn't believe—

Sharoosh! Like the slam of a teacher's wooden ruler slapping a daydreaming student's desk, tranquility instantly turned to terror. Every nerve ending in Roy's body began screaming in fear.

Something yanked his right wing.

Now, he was spinning out of control.

The ground became a blurry whirlpool of gray.

A few feathers brushed across his face.

Bart's voice shrieked in his ear. "Roy! Keep flapping your wings!"

He gasped.

Was that aluminum shimmering in the moonlight?

"My wing—lots of feathers are gone."

His right side felt weaker.

"Just keep flapping!" Bart pleaded.

This was it. He was going to die.

He pushed and twisted for his life.

For what seemed like hours.

The ground was getting closer.

Closer . . .

Closer . . .

He closed his eyes and waited for his certain death.

Still flapping all the while, though he questioned why.

Just give up, he thought.

Relieve your back of this useless pain.

You can't flap your way out of this one.

Accept your fate.

He forced his wings down one last time.

No more, he thought.

He squeezed his eyes shut and prepared for the end.

All he could hear was silence.

Then, he noticed. He no longer felt like a freshly spun top. And the wind had stopped tickling his right ear. Was it working? He pushed and twisted again, and dared to peek. With another push, the whirlpool was gone—the ground, once again, in a harmonious state.

Roy caught a glimpse of Bart nearby. "Stop flapping and lean to your left," he said.

Roy glided to his left. "See the parking lot?" Bart asked.

"Yeah."

"That's where you are going to land. Steady your wings and ease down. I'm right behind you."

Roy fought to keep his wings even. He wasn't far from the ground at all, but far enough to do some serious damage if he lost control. His speed was scary fast, and the parking lot asphalt disappeared into the darkness as he whizzed past surrounding buildings and signs.

"Drop your legs NOW." Bart's voice commanded.

Thump . . . scriissshhhh. It was too late. Roy only managed to get his legs out enough to drag them across the asphalt. He rolled forward onto his vest and came to a jarring stop, right before his chin had the chance to slam to the ground.

He heard Bart's footsteps rapidly approaching from behind. "You okay, kid?" He helped Roy to his feet. "I was afraid you hadn't seen that tree. No worries, we need to get out of here." Bart gripped the back of Roy's vest, and the two friends rushed behind a nearby building.

"Let's get you out of this and see what you did." Bart hastily removed Roy's flyer and leaned it against the building. "Looks like your knees will need some bandages. Anything hurt?" he asked. "Talk to me, kid."

"It was a tree? I hit a tree?"

"Yeah, that big pine, close to the pond," Bart said. "You were looking at the deer, and that ole tree caught you by surprise."

"I'm sorry," Roy began with a shaky voice. "I've ruined everything."

"Sorry? What for? Did my own stories of near misses and careless crashes mean nothing to you?" Bart asked with his usual smirk. "I've caused much worse than this. What matters is you got yourself out of the mess you put yourself into . . . and that's more than I can say for a lot of people."

Roy turned away from Bart. He was glad he had his goggles on—they hid the tears pooling in his eyes. "But it wasn't supposed to be like this."

"What was it supposed to be like?" Bart asked. "Like something out of a superhero novel? Hate to break it to you, kid, life doesn't work that way. That's why books like that are found in the fiction section."

Roy turned around and faced Bart. "I guess I should've known something would go wrong," Roy said. "I wanted everything to be perfect."

"Nothing wrong with striving for the best," Bart

shrugged. "But perfection—life doesn't allow that." The two friends shared a glance, looked over at Roy's crippled flyer, and both let out a relieved chuckle.

"We have to get out of here." Bart peeked around the edge of the building. "It's too far for you to walk. If I can get on this roof, I can fly home and then pick you up with my truck." He grabbed and shook one of the building's old drainpipes. "This will do."

Roy didn't like the sound of Bart's idea. "I can walk. I'm fine."

"No, kid. Can't leave the flyers for that long. And your knees are in pretty bad shape." Bart checked the straps on his flyer and lowered his googles. "Sit down right here."

"I'm supposed to stay here . . . alone?"

"I shouldn't be more than a few minutes," Bart said, seeming to be all business. "Looks like the fall damaged your headset. Maybe it still works though."

Roy flicked the on and off switch several times, pressing the speaker firmly against his ear. Nothing came through, not even static. "I guess it's broken."

"It's no big deal." Bart placed one foot against the brick wall and wrapped both hands around the rusty drainpipe. "The sooner I get out of here, the sooner I'll have you back safe and sound." Roy watched the Soaring

Fantom, hand-over-hand and step-by-step, make his way up the two-story wall. His winged ascent looked like a scene straight out of a superhero novel. Bart is wrong, Roy thought. Life did allow moments of perfection to slip through its meddling fingers.

Once on the roof, Bart offered up a few final words before taking flight. "I'll be back before you know it."

Yeah . . . right, Roy thought. He knew that no matter how quickly Bart returned, his absence would seem like forever. He didn't dare leave his spot to watch his friend fly away. He was too afraid to move. Roy was all alone, and there was nothing left to do but bring his burning knees to his face and curl up like a ball.

Strange noises filled the air. Were they the sounds of people, or wild animals? Roy worried—what if they were coming to get him? How helpless he must look. His parents would freak out if they knew what their little boy had gotten himself into. He could see his mom sobbing and his dad shaking his head in disgust and disappointment. They could never know about this—ever.

What made him think he could fly anyway? He was just a kid. He should be home, in bed, where it's safe. Even better, he should be on his way to the Grand Canyon right now, but his lie had brilliantly stopped that from happening. Now he was hiding behind a building after almost falling to his tragic death. He wanted nothing more than to be home—a place, for now, that felt light-years away.

CHAPTER 21

THE FINAL HOUR

Roy's eyes released the first in a line of tears. Many others soon followed, and by the time the headlights on Bart's truck revealed his pitiful situation, his eyes were almost swollen shut. Roy didn't care how childish he looked. He sprung to his feet and waved his arms desperately like the sole survivor of a shipwreck castaway for months on some uncharted island.

"Get in the car. I'll get the flyer," Bart said, jogging towards him. Roy didn't waste any time. He hopped in the front seat and waited while Bart packed the flyer between the gaps of an otherwise overstuffed truck. Within seconds, they were heading back to the safety of their neighborhood.

Neither friend had much to say during the brief ride through town. Roy stared out the passenger window.

The view, once again, appeared uninteresting. He found comfort in what he saw passing by him. He felt safe.

He looked up at the sky and back at Bart. Not in a billion years could he have ever dreamed of a summer like this one. One could say that he had gotten his mountaintop view. And the sharks. And the free fall. And a zip through the jungle. Except, instead of watching from the safe side of the glass, he'd stared directly into death's face and caught a whiff of its breath, which was much more than he had bargained for. But, as strange as it sounded, he wouldn't change one second of it. Because now, he had a ruler from which to measure all future risks. His was much longer than his parents', but plenty short of stupid. No matter what, he would have it for the rest of his life, and that made him happy.

"It's good to see you smiling," Bart said as he parked the truck in his driveway. "I was starting to worry about you."

"Who me? I'm great," Roy said.

"Let's get in the house and take a look at those knees." Roy followed Bart through the garage door and into the living room. "Sit here." Bart patted the top of one of the few boxes remaining. "I'll go get the first aid kit."

Roy grimaced his way onto the box. His knees didn't want to bend. Shirley nudged her head underneath his hand. He looked around the room and filled the emptiness with the time he and Bart had shared together. The smile on his face grew bigger. For weeks, he'd been dreading the end of this adventure. Of course, he would miss Bart. And he hoped Bart would miss him. But his friend had to move on, and so did he. That was the thing about adventures—they had to end, because if they lasted forever, they wouldn't be worth pursuing. The way he saw it, adventures were sort of like birthday cake. There's nothing better than a corner piece smothered in buttercream flowers. But if he went to a birthday party every day, he would get sick of cake and start craving vegetables. And he never wanted that to happen.

Bart's footsteps echoed down the stairwell. "It's not the best kit I have, but it'll do." He rolled up Roy's jeans and inspected the damage. "They're not as bad as I thought they'd be."

"They hardly hurt anymore." Roy cringed at the sight of his bright red blood.

Bart cleaned and bandaged the wounds like a pro. "Just wear jeans for a while and no one will be the wiser."

"I've always got some type of scrape or bruise," Roy said. "My mom says it comes with being a boy. She won't give them a second look."

Bart headed towards the kitchen. "Don't move, I have something for you." Bart returned from the kitchen with one hand behind his back. "Close your eyes." For the last time, Roy did exactly as his friend instructed. Bart placed something in his hand. "I want you to have this—as a token of our summer together."

Roy looked down at his hand now holding an Invisoscript. "I can't take this. It's your invention. You should be the only one using it."

"Take it . . . I insist. I have plenty, and you've earned it." Bart closed Roy's hand around the pen. "I know you will never share it with anyone. Besides, you need something other than some scarred knees to remind you of our summer together."

"But you don't have anything to remember me by," Roy said.

"Sure I do," Bart said. "I have your right wing. I'm going to hang it in my workshop at my new house, damaged and all. Not only will it remind me of our time together, it will make me smile when I think of what a trustworthy and brave friend you were. Besides, I have a photographic memory . . . remember?"

"Thanks for the pen . . . for everything." Roy stood up and rolled his jeans down. "But, I could never forget this summer, even without a photographic memory."

"Yeah, same here," Bart said. "And maybe one day, I'll be able to fly far enough to soar right over your house. Then, no telling what can happen."

"If anyone can do it, you can." Roy gave Bart a final high five. "Thanks for the best summer of my life, Soaring Fantom."

For the last time, Roy patted Shirley on the head, then left through Bart's side door. All he could manage was a straight-legged trot home. He winced up the fire escape and carefully wrapped the rope around the branch so that it looked like no one had ever used it. Once safe in his room, he reached far under his bed and pulled out a wooden box he'd made in Boy Scouts. Roy opened it and arranged a secure spot for the Invisoscript among his other secret treasures. He returned the box to its hidden location and lay down on his bed.

As the summer nights played back in his mind, none of them seemed real. Roy considered the possibility that Melonie would awake him at any second, only for him to discover it had all been a dream. His throbbing knees, though, screamed otherwise.

Without a doubt, he had become friends with a

superhero who gave him the power to fly. So, he hadn't soared as far as he planned; he had still reached his true goal. He was no longer the Charles Royston Winklesteen III sitting at his desk dreaming of a more interesting, confident, and courageous version of himself.

And even though his poster wouldn't be as awesome as he had hoped it would be, he didn't care. Besides, visiting the southwest was a perfectly respectable summer adventure, and he was actually looking forward to spending time with his family. After all the nerve-racking nights with Bart, he welcomed the heaping dose of overprotection, sisterly admiration, and parental love the trip was sure to offer. Heck, he might even let Melonie pick out the pictures for his poster. Everyone at school would see images of the Grand Canyon, cactuses, and donkeys, but he would see the two winged figures he'd drawn with his Invisoscript before he glued on the pictures. Who cares if no one knew he had flown like a bird? He knew. And he had the wings to prove it. He couldn't feel them, and he couldn't see them, but they were there.

And along with his ruler of risk, he now had the tools to tackle middle school and beyond. He was ready to take chances—and not just the kind that involved swimming with sharks or leaping off a roof—but the really frightening kind. Like talking to the popular kids, or speaking up in class, or running for student council, or telling your best friend that you really don't like soccer, or not apologizing for the fact you are a nerd that likes playing with Legos. It all sounded scary, but Roy wasn't afraid anymore. After all, he was a nightlifer, and he knew the darkness would always help him find his way.

With one last jolt of energy, Roy retrieved his box of secret treasures and clutched the Invisoscript. He faced the wall next to his bed and sketched the silhouette of a flying figure soaring past the moon. Next, he drew a smaller figure right below it. He stared at his drawing until he could only see it in his mind. Completely satisfied, he put the box back and crawled under the covers.

He looked up at his window and let out a mischievous snicker. Now, he officially knew there were others who preferred moonlight to sunshine. And, like Bart, they were probably doing stuff daylifers only dreamt of doing.

Oh . . . the possibilities!

Good thing his nighttime calendar was wide open.

ABOUT THE AUTHOR

Sally Dill grew up in Louisiana and has degrees in architecture and interior design. She lives with her husband and two children in North Carolina. She has been a nightlifer for as long as she can remember.

Made in the USA
Coppell, TX
11 December 2020

44418800R00121